A YOUNG A[...]

SEVENTH DIMENSION

INTERNATIONAL
BOOK AWARDS
FINALIST
IntlBookAwards.com

LORILYN ROBERTS

THE
DOOR

A YOUNG ADULT FANTASY

SEVENTH DIMENSION
BOOK I

THE DOOR

LORILYN ROBERTS

PRAISE FOR LORILYN ROBERTS

THE SEVENTH DIMENSION SERIES HAS WON OVER THIRTY BOOK AWARDS

"A colorful portrait painted with entertaining characters, lively dialogue, and beautifully adorned with a profound message. The life-like journey evokes tears and cheers, filling the reader with delight."

— -JANET PEREZ ECKLES, BEST-SELLING AUTHOR

"Dazzling imagery, like a Biblical *Alice in Wonderland"*

— -ROGER HUNT, ROGER HUNT MUSIC

"A heartwarming story with lovable animal characters, a stirring heroine, and a king's love for his children—truly pleasing for young and old alike."

— -HANNAH BOMBARDIER (AGE 17)

"...Wonderful Counselor

Mighty God

Everlasting Father

Prince of Peace

Isaiah 9:6

To Harry

Who told me I was a daughter of the King

— "TIME IS AN ALLUSION UNTIL GOD'S APPOINTED TIME." – LORILYN ROBERTS

INTRODUCTION

"A spiritual kingdom lies all about us, enclosing us, embracing us, altogether within reach of our inner selves, waiting for us to recognize it. God Himself is here waiting our response to His Presence. This eternal world will come alive to us the moment we begin to reckon upon its reality."— A. W. Tozer, *The Pursuit of God*

The Door is the first book in the six-book *Seventh Dimension Series* that combines contemporary, historical, and fantasy elements into a Christian coming-of-age story. A curse put on Shale Snyder, because of a secret, shrouds her with insecurity and fear. Following suspension from school, Shale's best friend isn't allowed to see her anymore, and she feels abandoned by her family. When a stray dog befriends her, she follows it into the woods. There she discovers a door that leads to a secret garden.

PROLOGUE

 DIARY ENTRY MANY YEARS LATER

"Long ago, a magical king was born in a kingdom where animals talked and intellect sparred with spirituality. It was a time when truth transcended culture, forgiveness won battles, and love conquered a young girl's heart."

But lest I get ahead of myself, let me start from the beginning—which happened a long, long, long time ago. So long ago, I barely remember the beginning of my journey to the *Seventh Dimension*.

CHAPTER 1

DARK SECRET OF SHALE SNYDER

I hid in a closet underneath the stairs—my safe house. Nobody would find me here. The ceiling was too low. I don't think anyone knew about the small room but me.

After the accident, the closet became my friend. I wanted to avoid Judd, who came over to visit Chumana. She was not my sister but we lived together.

The door creaked as I turned the handle. I held my breath and peered through the tiny slit. Moving shadows darkened the room. Judd, Rachel, and Chumana stared into a small brown shoebox.

Chumana burst out crying. "I hate Shale."

I cringed. She already hated me anyway, ever since my mother and me moved in with them a few months earlier.

Rachel stood and recited a Jewish prayer. "*Barukh shem k'vod malkhuto l'olam va'ed.* Blessed is the name of his glorious kingdom forever and ever." With her unkempt hair, puffy red eyes, and flushed face, I barely recognized my best friend.

"Why are you praying?" Judd snapped. "We aren't here to pray."

"Accidents happen," Rachel said.

"She should be cursed," Judd exploded.

"Don't say that," Rachel said.

"How do you know it was an accident?" Chumana asked.

I looked away. I couldn't listen. My whole body shook—what kind of curse?

Judd's voice cracked. "I demand she tell us what happened."

The three twelve-year-olds sat silently for a moment before Rachel responded. "She fell down the stairs with Fifi, and she's afraid."

I swallowed hard.

Judd pulled his uncle's Atlanta Braves cap over his eyes and clinched his hand into a fist. "I hope Shale never has any friends—for the rest of her life." He covered his face and sobbed.

I bit my fingernail holding back tears. I'd never heard a boy cry. Could his curse come true?

Chumana's red hair matched her fiery temper. "That's not enough of a curse. She already doesn't have any friends."

"I'm her friend," Rachel said. "Accidents happen."

Rachel lived two buildings down from us in the Hope Garden Apartments. Would she still be my friend if I told her the truth? I didn't just fall—it was what I was doing when I fell. I was too afraid. I rubbed my swollen ankle, a reminder of my foolishness. The doctor hoped it would heal, but Fifi lay in the box.

Probably God hated me, too. If I told the truth, everyone would hate me. I couldn't even tell my mother. My father—he left me long ago.

TWO YEARS LATER

. . .

I felt a hand reach underneath my blue skirt. I spun around on my toes. Students in the crowded hallway blended into a blur of anonymity. Hurried bodies shoved past. Am I going crazy? Did I imagine it? I scanned faces and froze each one, like a snapshot with a camera.

Rachel was waiting at the hall lockers. "Shale, why are you standing there? Come on or you'll be late to class."

I walked towards her as the bell rang.

She furrowed her brow. "Are you okay?"

"I'm fine." I smiled, pretending nothing had happened. I'd think about it later. "Did you finish your analysis of *As You Like It*?"

Rachel's brown eyes bulged. "Is it due today?"

"Here's mine. You can take a quick look."

"Oh, thanks, Shale. I hate Shakespeare anyway. No copying, promise. Just a peek."

"It's no different from reading Spark Notes on the web," I quipped.

When we walked into English class at Garden High School, I sat in the seat closest to the door and stared out into the darkened hallway. Who did it? What would I do if I caught him? Mrs. Wilkes's voice brought me back to reality as she recited from a Shakespearean play.

"All the world's a stage.
And all the men and women merely players
They have their exits and their entrances
And one man in his time plays many parts
His acts being seven ages."

What was my part? At fourteen, did I have one yet?

Later in the afternoon, I tripped while stepping off the school bus, scattering my books over the ground. My bum ankle from the accident two years earlier would catch at the worst possible moment—what I considered my eternal punishment.

Scrambling to pick them up, I wiped the red Georgia clay off my math book. The bus waited long enough to make sure it wouldn't run me over before pulling away.

"Hey, wait up, ya'll." I walked faster to catch up as Rachel stopped, but Chumana and Judd kept going. We still lived in the same apartment complex on the south side of Atlanta.

"If you used a backpack, you wouldn't have dropped your books," Rachel chided me.

"Mine broke." I scanned Rachel's back. "Where's yours?"

"I did my homework at school." Rachel waved a thick book with strange-looking letters in the air. "This is all I needed."

"Can you read that stuff?"

"Sure," Rachel laughed, "but I don't know what it means. You could too if I taught you." Rachel flipped to the first page. "You start on this side." Her finger pointed to a line of Hebrew, and she ran her finger across the page from right to left.

"Really?"

"Yes." Rachel giggled. "So who reads backwards, the English or the Jews?"

"I'd say the Jews. I can say that since I'm not Jewish, right?"

"Why not?"

"Writing would sure be easier if English was right to left. I wouldn't smear my words."

Rachel nodded. "I forget you're left-handed. It's crazy, isn't it—like the Brits drive on the left side and we drive on the right."

We walked for a while not saying anything. I glanced at my friend with her striking olive skin, almond brown eyes, and brown hair. "Do you like being Jewish?"

"Yeah, I guess. I don't know any different."

"I wish I was Jewish."

"Why?" Rachel asked.

"It would be neat to be able to say I was something."

"You could go to church," Rachel suggested.

"Mom and Remi would never go. Every time they talk about God or anything religious, they end up fighting."

Rachel flinched. "That's too bad. By the way, thanks for your help with English."

"You're welcome." I switched my books to the left. I hated the long walk home, especially since we now lived farther away. The new unit we moved into when Remi and mother married was at the very back by the woods.

Rachel frowned, noticing my musings. "What's it like having a father now?"

I bit my lip. "At least I have my own bedroom and don't have to share with Chumana."

"That's good," Rachel agreed. "How did you ever end up living with her anyway?"

"Mother didn't have any money when we moved to Atlanta. She found an ad that Chumana's mother placed in the *Atlanta Constitution* looking for a roommate. It was a cheap place to live."

I eyed Judd and Chumana ahead of us. "What are they talking about? They have been spending a lot of time together."

Rachel lowered her voice. "I know."

"Maybe they deserve each other."

Rachel edged up closer to me and spoke in a whisper. "You never knew your father, right?"

"No." I double clutched my books that now seemed heavier. "Mother couldn't wait to marry Remi after being divorced for so many years. Then she cried all night when they returned from their honeymoon. I wondered why, but I was too afraid to ask."

"Maybe it was a bad honeymoon," Rachel chortled.

"Silly you. How can you have a bad honeymoon?"

"I don't know," Rachel replied. "I'm sure it's happened."

"I hardly knew Remi the day they married."

"It's hard to imagine what it would be like to be at your own parent's wedding. I mean, it might be funny if it could happen."

"Like *Back to the Future*?" My thoughts darkened. "How would you like having a stepfather you didn't know?"

Rachel shook her head. "I wouldn't."

I'd never confided in anyone about my past, but now I couldn't stop. "Presents arrive twice a year from North York. I don't remember anything about my father. One day he left and never returned."

"I can't imagine what that would be like," Rachel said.

"Sometimes I get angry."

Rachel's eyes widened. "About what?"

"Mother didn't ask how I felt about her remarrying."

We walked in silence as my words hung in the air. I kicked a rock on the sidewalk, and it skipped into the gutter. Rachel's warm nature was comforting. She came from such a perfect family, or it seemed. I'd tell her things I wouldn't tell anyone else.

Voices from the past mocked me. "Do I walk like a chicken?"

Rachel laughed. "No, you don't walk like a chicken."

"Do I have big lips?"

"Big lips?" Rachel stopped and stared at me surprised. "No."

"You don't think so? Every time I wet them with my tongue, I worry I'm making them fat—so I was told."

Rachel examined my fair face. I pretended not to notice. "You're beautiful. Who would say such mean things?"

I didn't want to tell her. What was the point in making him look bad?

Rachel reached out and grabbed a couple of strands of my hair, flipping them over my shoulder. "I love your green eyes and long brown hair. I wish mine wasn't wavy with all the humidity. I use an iron to straighten it, but it doesn't stay that way for long."

Rachel giggled. "Guys love long, straight hair."

"Remi wants me to call him dad, but that seems weird."

A few feet in front of us, Chumana knelt on the sidewalk.

Rachel squinted. "What are they looking at?"

When we got closer, I could see an earthworm wiggling on the sidewalk. A few weeks after Christmas, it was the wrong time of year for creepy crawlers.

"It's probably cold," I said.

Judd lifted his foot to squash it.

"Wait," I demanded.

Judd glared at me.

"Why kill it?" I asked.

He leaned down and picked it up, dangling the worm a few inches above the sidewalk. "Have you ever dissected one of these?"

I shook my head.

He stiffened. "I should make you squish it between your delicate fingers."

I stared at the worm. Judd dropped it on the sidewalk. As he started to smash it again, I leaned over and shoved him. "Just leave it alone."

Judd's face turned beet red. "Don't ever push me again. You hear me?"

I nodded. My knees spasmed like a jack-in-the-box.

His icy eyes ripped at my soul. "You don't like squishing worms, but you killed my puppy."

Rachel said, "Get over it. You sound so hateful."

Chumana glared through her thick, black-rimmed glasses. "Judd is right, though, Rachel. Don't you remember?"

"I remember," Rachel whispered.

My heart raced as I picked up the worm—its slimy body was cold to the touch—and stuck it in my pocket.

Judd shook his head and stomped off.

I urged Rachel and Chumana. "You two go on. I'll see you tomorrow."

Rachel nodded. They continued walking, leaving me alone.

After wrapping the worm in some brown leaves, I placed it on a warmer corner of the concrete. When I lifted my eyes, I saw her for the first time. She was mostly white with a few brown spots, medium size, and thick fur covered her soft body for the cold Atlanta winters. She sat on the sidewalk wagging her fluffy tail.

As I started to approach her, she stood and limped backwards. Despite her natural beauty, the scruffy creature was dirty. Her floppy short ears had mangy spots, and her almond brown eyes appeared crusty. If she belonged to someone or was lost, the owner wasn't taking very good care of her. A warm fuzziness filled my heart. Before I could get too close, however, the dog turned and ran away.

CHAPTER 2

S USPENSION

"Who Am I?

when no one sees
   when no one loves
   when no one understands
   when no one hears
   when no one cares about

Me."

I closed my diary, locked it, and set it aside. I hid the key under my pillow. Sleepy dreams visited me, but the diary called my name. I flipped the light switch back on, grabbed the diary from my nightstand, and stashed it in a dark corner of the bookshelf.

Another book, *The Donkey and the King,* caught my attention. I'd not looked at it for a long time. I pulled it off the bookshelf and flipped through its worn, crinkled pages.

Even when I was younger, I felt sorry for the donkey. Baruch ran away from the stable and got lost. A sheep found him and took him to meet a powerful king. Much-Afraid, the dog in the story, looked like that stray dog I saw when I came home from school. The resemblance surprised me.

I set the book back on the bookshelf. Along the baseboard, a straight pin clung to the wood. Mother must have dropped it when she fixed my backpack. I scooted over and picked it up. The pin was three or four inches long. I rubbed my finger along the sharp magnetic tip and stuffed it into my sweater pocket.

Then I climbed back into bed and let my eyes adjust to the blackness. Dark creatures danced on the walls in the moonlight. They often visited me at night before I drifted off to sleep, like cartoon characters that never slept.

The bell rang and the ninth grade stragglers found their seats. Mrs. Wilkes took roll, followed by an in-depth critique of Shakespeare's play, *As You Like It.* She was a diminutive old woman, boxy with skinny legs and an overpowering voice. The class listened politely, though most could have cared less about the finer points of literary criticism.

When it came to competing with iPads and iPods and iPhones and Blackberries, critiquing seemed tedious unless downloaded on a Kindle, but Mrs. Wilkes was too old fashioned to permit them in class. Disheveled papers covered her desk.

My heart skipped when she announced my name, Shale Snyder. Clearing her throat, she began. "Would one be better off never to love and avoid being hurt? Does love always make one happy? *As You Like*

It has its roots in Greek literature, although written by Shakespeare between 1598 and 1600..." Her voice trailed off as she read a few more lines to herself. Then, with one fell swoop, she threw my paper in the trash. "This is too well written to be original. I'm sure Shale copied it off the web. I'm not going to read it."

Thirty sets of eyes shifted to me, and my face and neck felt hot. Mrs. Wilkes's beady eyes pulsated. No one moved. If I dropped the straight pin hidden in my sweater pocket, the room would have heard it ping on the floor.

After an unbearable silence, she added, "We'll deal with this later." She dug in her pile for another report.

Anything else that happened was a blur, except the ringing of the bell. I ran out the door with Mrs. Wilkes's voice trailing behind me. "Shale Snyder, I need to talk to you."

Before I got more than a few feet down the hall, I felt a hand reach up my skirt. I spun. Angry fireballs surged through my popping veins. My eyes dashed back and forth, examining faces and moving bodies in the crowded hallway. There he was—right in front of me, snaking through the maze. The boy wore a red shirt and Atlanta Braves cap.

I shoved students out of my way and heard gasps and curse words as I splayed bodies on the floor. A teacher in a lab coat ducked back into her classroom. When the guilty one turned his head, the nerve endings on my spine tingled. I lunged forward.

Reaching into my sweater pocket, I pulled out the straight pin and stabbed it into his back. Judd winced in pain. I jammed my hand as hard as I could and then pulled out the pin. My hand felt numb, and the pin slipped out of my fingers and fell onto the floor.

I looked around. Shocked students stood frozen, mouths gaping. Judd groaned as he hunched over. A wet splotch grew on his back, soaking through his shirt. It looked like blood. Did I hurt him that badly? My heart raced.

"You little witch!" Judd shrieked. I started to hyperventilate. Tripping over students, I hurried to my next class, scrambling out of sight as he yelled profanities.

As I neared the gymnasium, I still felt his hand touching me.

Seeing the blood on his back made me dizzy. I stood outside the gym entrance breathless. What would happen if the kids reported it? How much did the lab teacher see? What would Remi, my stepfather, do if he found out?

I coiled my hands around the metal flagpole. The late bell rang. I pulled out my cell phone as time ticked. I was already twenty minutes late. I leaned my head against the pole. Be calm. This was my last class. Just open the door.

Inside the girl's dressing room, I headed for my locker. The other students were already outside. As I reached for the metal handle, I noticed the door was already open. Pulling on it, I almost yanked the door off its hinges. Where was my uniform? I checked every corner—it was missing.

"Are you looking for something?"

I turned to see Chumana. A wicked smile crossed her lips, and her smirk irritated me.

"Yes. My gym outfit. Do you know where it is?"

"Try the toilet, doll," Chumana snickered. "Even though you don't live with me anymore, I can still make your life miserable—cursed." She ran out the gym door.

I bolted to the bathroom and checked the stalls. In the first one, a blue uniform floated in the commode. I pulled it out by the end that wasn't wet. Globs of water dropped back into the toilet. Holding it away from me as it dripped on the floor, I took it over to the sink. Yuck! The water splattered when I turned on the faucet.

Clicking heels approached. I expected to see Chumana, but instead, Mrs. Twiggs stood in the doorway—a left-behind Nazi. She wore her hair pulled back in a bun, and a navy pencil skirt clung to her skinny legs. Her black stockings and pointed shoes reminded me of a witch. Her steely eyes had far too much mascara.

She smacked a ruler in her hand. "Follow me to the office."

The running water had formed clouds of hot vapors. "Can I get my books?"

"Hurry," the principal demanded.

I shut off the water and examined my wet uniform. I didn't want it anyway. I'd make Chumana replace it—somehow. It wasn't enough to get even. I wanted payback.

Mrs. Twiggs pointed with the ruler for me to walk in front of her. The Nazi wanted nothing better than to see me expelled. I couldn't remember how many times I had been in her office. Too many students had tattled on me for ridiculous reasons. Sometimes I was in the wrong place at the wrong time.

On the way, another teacher stopped us. She and Mrs. Twiggs stepped aside and spoke in whispers. They occasionally made eye contact. I hated not knowing if they were talking about me. The whole time, Mrs. Twiggs smacked the ruler in her hand.

After a few minutes, we continued to the office, located in the adjoining building by the school entrance. I gasped when I opened the door. "Remi!"

He sat in a chair beside the lab teacher who had seen me in the hallway. I wasn't used to seeing my stepfather look so debonair in his business suit and red tie. Our eyes met before I glanced away. I took a seat as far from him as possible. What had the lab teacher told him?

"Mr. Heller, I'm Mrs. Twiggs, the principal. I'm sorry to call you away from work, but we need you to take Shale home. She's being suspended."

"For chasing a student in the hallway?"

"She attacked Judd Luster."

Remi rubbed the back of his neck, looking baffled. "Mrs. Gluck here told me what happened—that Shale chased a young man down the hallway and caused a commotion. Have you asked for her side of the story?"

Mrs. Twiggs snapped the ruler. "What's there to ask?"

When Remi didn't answer, she continued. "There's never an excuse for violence at school. If he offended her in some way, she should have reported it. There are proper channels for handling disputes between students. Using a deadly weapon isn't one of them."

"A weapon?" Remi asked.

I examined the wooden parquet tiles on the floor. Maybe he didn't hear that part.

Mrs. Twiggs stated matter-of-factly. "Shale has a history of issues dating back to first grade. I'll have a psychological assessment done as soon as possible. I'm suspending her from school until the testing is completed."

"Suspending me from school?" She ignored my question.

"Then we'll decide if she can return. Do you have any questions, Mr. Heller?"

Remi's face looked stunned.

Tears welled up in my eyes. He would never believe me. Did I want to tell him? I was embarrassed to talk about it. What was a psychological assessment anyway?

I zoned out as Mrs. Twiggs made mindless accusations about me—what a troubled kid I was and that I'd never amount to anything if someone didn't set me straight.

I didn't want to ride home with Remi and listen to him blow up at me in the car.

I vaguely heard Mrs. Twiggs addressing me, "Shale, do you have anything to add?"

"What?" I asked.

"Do you have anything to say?"

Sure. I had lots to say, but not to her, not to Remi, not to my mother. I felt like a bird trapped in a cage. I wanted to fly away and never return. I imagined myself so thick-skinned that nothing anyone said or did to me would hurt, but I wasn't like that.

"Do you have anything you want to add, Shale? We're waiting."

I looked at each of them, searching for a sympathetic ear. I shook my head. A teardrop fell on my hand as I covered my mouth with a fist to deafen my sobs.

"Thank you, Mr. Heller, for your prompt attention. I know you and Mrs. Heller recently married. I'd hoped things would get better for Shale with a father in the house. Perhaps it will take more time."

"He's not my father," I blurted out.

"What did you say, little lady?" the principal asked.

"Never mind, Mrs. Twiggs." Remi reached out to shake her hand. She stood blocking the door.

"Are we done?" Remi asked.

The principal didn't move.

"I promise to talk to Shale's mother about her behavior, Mrs. Twiggs. I'm sorry for all of this." His extended hand waited for a response.

After an awkward moment, she shoved her hand into his. "I've already contacted Doctor Silverstein. We'll do the testing in the next couple of days."

"As soon as possible would be appreciated so Shale doesn't miss too much school." Remi turned to me. "Grab your books, honey, and let's go."

"Can—can I go to the restroom?"

Remi glanced at Mrs. Twiggs.

She nodded. "Go ahead."

I rushed down the hall to the restroom and shoved open the door. It smacked into something on the other side. I stumbled into the bathroom and saw urinals lining the wall. Had I walked into the men's room? I spun around to make a quick exit— and collided into a bare-chested male. Judd's cold eyes met mine.

"Get out of my way," I screeched.

"Why are you in here?"

"I—I went into the wrong bathroom."

I glanced down, and in his hand was a blood-soaked paper towel. I shoved past him, but he grabbed me from behind and sunk his fingers into my shoulder.

"Let me go," I screamed.

I got away and ran out the door. Someday he's going to murder me because I killed his dog.

CHAPTER 3

S HALE FACES JUDGMENT

A knock on my bedroom door disturbed the silence. I closed the diary and hid it underneath the covers.

"Come in."

Mother walked in and sat on the side of my bed. Her puffy eyes betrayed dried tears. I overheard her and Remi behind closed doors arguing about me. Earlier in the day, when Remi brought me home, he ranted the whole time. When he got tired of letting off steam, he gave me the silent treatment, staring straight at the road, distant and angry. I wasn't sure I could ever connect with him, let alone allow him to be a father to me.

"Honey," she said. Mother twisted the knotted handkerchief in her lap, her bony knuckles white from tension. "How would you like to go live with your father for a while? Maybe it would be good for you to make that connection."

"My father?" I convinced myself she couldn't be serious, just desperate.

"Oh, never mind." She wistfully tossed her head aside, looking across the room, "You—you're so much like him. He couldn't get along with a fence post, let alone me. I don't want you to turn out like him—an alcoholic, hooked on drugs, wasting all that talent. Of course, I'm sure he's not like that now...."

A distant look of regret and sorrow shadowed her blood-shot eyes, hardened by the passage of time. She hated my father, what he did to her, how he deserted us on a dark street in Miami. I had heard the story many times. Mother wandered the streets looking for a stranger to take us in. Who wanted to put up a homeless mother and a crying baby?

Her raw emotions flared. "Why can't you behave at school and not cause us so much trouble? You want to destroy this marriage, too?" She dabbed her tears with a handkerchief. "I—I don't know how to love you. You push us away with your bad behavior, like you mean to hurt us."

I reminded her of a past she wanted to forget, especially when I looked a certain way, though I never knew what that way was. I had his eyes, his smile. If only I did have his talent, maybe I'd be worth something.

"You have no idea what I went through to keep you," she continued. "They wanted you."

"Who wanted me?" I asked.

"You were a ward of the state." Regaining her composure, warmth returned to her strained face. "Get some sleep, honey." She leaned over and whispered. "I want you to do well on the testing tomorrow." She kissed me on the forehead and left.

As she closed the door, her words echoed in my ears. She wanted me to do well to save her marriage. That was it. It was all about her. What about me? Shadows swept through my bedroom. Dancing shades of gray cartoon creatures covered my walls once again as I drifted off to sleep.

We crowded into the principal's office around a small oak table on the third day of testing. Why did I have to take the same test twice? I took the first one on Monday and then a similar test on Tuesday. Midway through the second one, I just filled in the blanks. I didn't care anymore.

Remi and my mother were to the right. Mrs. Twiggs sat across from me. The psychologist, Dr. Silverstein, was at the head of the table. Books lined the wall behind him. The voices of students rose and fell as they passed by the office doorway. The subdued lighting in the room darkened my optimism about the outcome. I hoped I wouldn't be expelled.

Remi had driven home from work to bring us. Mother dressed up more than usual and wore heavy make-up and high heels. Since I had been suspended, I didn't need to wear a dress, but I wore one anyway. I dabbed on enough make-up to cover a zit that had popped up overnight.

Staring through the frosted glass out the office door, I wished I were somewhere else. The room became uncomfortably quiet as we waited to begin. Two sets of official-looking papers labeled "Shale Snyder" were stacked in front of Dr. Silverstein. He reminded me of an eccentric scientist, wearing glasses that were too big. His bushy eyebrows stuck out and I wanted to pluck them and watch him cringe.

Mrs. Twiggs turned on a tape recorder and gave the perfunctory greetings. "Doctor Silverstein, our school psychologist here at Garden High School, has conducted an examination of Shale's psychological, intellectual, and cognitive abilities. He's a leading authority on 'troubled kids' and has prepared a report to share with us."

Mrs. Twiggs readjusted the tape recorder to the center of the table. "I was going to set up this meeting for next week, but because the parents of Shale Snyder insisted we hold this hearing as soon as possible, I re-arranged my busy schedule to accommodate them."

"Appreciate that," Remi said. Mother nodded.

Mrs. Twiggs opened a plastic packet and dumped the contents out on the table. "This is a pin that was found on the hall floor where Shale attacked Judd Luster."

Mother examined the straight pin. "I wondered where this went to. Shale, where did you find it?"

"It was on the floor in my bedroom, against the wall."

"I must have dropped it when I fixed the zipper on your backpack." She picked up the pin and rubbed it between her fingers. Mother eyed me questioningly, but didn't say anything else. She then turned to Dr. Silverstein. "What about the testing?"

Remi reached over and grabbed Mother's hand. "Do you have the results?"

Dr. Silverstein flipped through his documents to look for the pertinent information. He adjusted his glasses and began. "Shale Snyder was referred to me for evaluation following an incident at school. She has a long history of juvenile delinquency. Our first intervention occurred when she failed first grade."

The doctor took a sip of coffee before continuing. "However, Shale did successfully repeat the grade, but continued to exhibit behavioral problems when she entered high school, including disrespect for authority, inability to follow rules, painting graffiti on the school hallways, cheating, plagiarism, and initiating fights, which, as I alluded to, resulted in a student requiring medical treatment. The latter event is what prompted this psychological evaluation."

"I never drew on the walls," I protested.

Remi admonished me to be quiet with his eyes.

Dr. Silverstein continued. "I performed cognitive testing twice. The second set of testing was done to validate the results of the first test."

I wished someone had explained that to me.

He stopped reading, looked up, and twitched his eyebrows. "Mr. and Mrs. Heller, the second test contradicts the first test. I couldn't come to definite conclusions."

He slid the papers over to Mother. "On this test she was a genius, scoring 150 plus. On the second test, a day later, she was, how should I say it, she had an I.Q of less than 70—borderline retardation."

Dr. Silverstein leaned toward them. "How should I say this? Nothing on the second test validates the first test. She scored the exact opposite on all portions—except for one thing."

"What's that?"

"She has a gift."

"What gift?" Remi asked. "The only talent I see is her tendency to get into trouble."

"Hardly," Dr. Silverstein said. "There's a pattern in these tests I can't explain."

"What pattern?" Mother asked.

"She has a gift. Maybe it's art, writing, music, mathematics, language—I'm not sure, but in time, we'll know. Gifted kids have special needs to reach their God-given potential."

"Gifted?" Mrs. Twiggs fumed. "She's a juvenile delinquent going around hurting students with pins and turning in plagiarized work. She could have killed a student. Imagine the lawsuit we'd have on our hands."

The clock struck three. Soon school would let out. I had misjudged Dr. Silverstein. I should have taken the second test more seriously.

Mrs. Twiggs looked like a teakettle ready to explode. "I don't see how you came to that conclusion."

I imagined steam dripping from her nose.

"I'm not finished." Dr. Silverstein took another sip of his black coffee. "That is the I.Q. portion of the test."

The principal rubbed her forehead and opened her purse, pulling out Tylenol. "What are your recommendations?"

"I'd recommend counselor intervention on a weekly basis to work through some deeper issues. I wouldn't expel her from school."

Mother heaved a sigh.

"No expulsion!" Mrs. Twiggs's face turned multiple shades of raspberry. "She must be expelled. In fact, I demand her expulsion."

"I'm giving you my recommendation," Dr. Silverstein said.

Mrs. Twiggs's mouth twitched. The Tylenol must not be working.

She stood and paced around the room, muttering under her breath. Without recourse, defeated, she gave in reluctantly.

"Very well, Doctor Silverstein. This isn't what I wanted, but I'll submit your recommendation to the school board. If anything happens that puts students at risk, though, you will be responsible. I completely disagree with you, I might add."

Her position and opinion couldn't have been clearer.

"One more chance for this troubled young lady," she continued, "though a three-day suspension is mandatory."

Even after the missed classes with the testing? What a bummer.

"But, mark my word, if she does anything else to cause any disruption at this school, she'll be expelled immediately. Do you understand, Mr. and Mrs. Heller?"

"We understand, Mrs. Twiggs," Remi said. "I promise you, she won't do anything else. I'll make sure of that." He turned towards me, but I refused to look at him.

"Great. I'll hold you to that. Good luck," she added. "You'll need it."

"I'd be willing to do some counseling with Shale in the meantime," Dr. Silverstein offered.

"We don't need anything more from you," Mrs. Twiggs said. "We'll consider counseling later."

The meeting was over, although the tape recorder was still running. What kind of counseling?

Mrs. Twiggs thanked Dr. Silverstein glibly and headed towards the door.

Mother asked. "Can I have my pin back?"

"Have your pin back? No," Mrs. Twiggs stated firmly. "I need this as evidence for the future. You will be back."

Not if I could help it. Was it legal for her to keep the pin? Mother and Remi didn't say anything to protest. I lagged behind as the rest of them walked outside. Quickly, I flipped the switch off on the tape recorder and grabbed the cassette. Who used these ancient things anyway? One less person.

CHAPTER 4

T HE DOOR

I stacked my books on the dining room table—Latin, history, English, science, math—which one did I want to do first? I shrugged. Suspension for three days made me feel like a juvenile delinquent.

What would I say when I faced Judd again? Rumors filtered through the school that I went into the boy's restroom. Kids snickered and pointed at me in the school hallway before the suspension. No matter what others said, I wasn't going to tell anyone why I attacked him. If I did, I might as well hang my dirty underwear on the school flagpole.

Students' imaginations would conjure up the worst—soon they would have me sleeping with him. Staring ahead blankly at the stack of books, I couldn't focus long enough to pull one out and start.

The doorbell rang. I walked over and opened the door, and a man in a UPS uniform held a small package in his hand. I glanced behind him and saw a brown truck idling. I signed for the package, and as he headed back to his truck, I noticed a white envelope clinging to the doorstep. I picked it up and tucked it under my arm.

As the UPS truck pulled away, I glanced at the return address on the package. My father would keep sending me Christmas presents after all. I closed the door and headed to the sofa. Then I read the return address on the note—Rachel Franco. Why would Rachel have slipped a note in the door? I set the package down to open hers first.

I read the handwriting silently. "Dear Shale, I'm writing you because I couldn't tell you in person. Mother and Father don't want me to be friends with you anymore. They think you're bad for me. I know you wouldn't have done what you did to Judd without good reason. It doesn't seem fair because we've been good friends for so long, but I must obey my parents. I can't walk with you home from the bus or talk to you in class. You will always be my best friend. Signed, Rachel Franco. P.S. I'll be praying for you as I always do. God has a purpose in this—I hope."

I read the letter three times, slowly, thinking about each sentence. Yes, she would always be my best friend, too. I knew she prayed because she was Jewish. However, what purpose could God have in this? If he did, he had a strange way of showing it.

I threw the letter down and stared at the bare walls that still needed pictures. Bed sheets covered the windows. The flat-screen television belonged to Remi. I was forbidden to touch it—he was sure I would break it. Stashed against the wall were duplicate wedding gifts mother had yet to return.

Rachel was my only friend. She would come over at least once a week—bring me a good book to read, or I'd help her with a school assignment, but I was never allowed to visit her. I never knew why. Mother always gave some lame excuse. I'd never met her parents. Now I wouldn't have even one friend at school. I wished I'd told Rachel the truth.

The room was quiet except for the leaky commode upstairs Remi promised Mother he would fix. A scratching noise on the backdoor annoyed me. What could that be? My legs were too heavy to get up and check.

I examined the UPS package from my father. The small box looked ordinary. I tore off the brown paper and found inside a white flimsy box—the kind of box that usually contains a breakable. I opened it carefully so as not to shake it.

The box contained a light green, blue, and purple ceramic egg. The colors blended into one another, etched by a skilled artisan. I carefully opened the egg. Underneath a layer of fluffy cotton was a family of rabbits—a mother rabbit with three small babies.

My heart sank. The bunnies were broken. Only one of the rabbits was whole, but even it had a chipped ear. A baby had a missing head, and another had a broken leg. The mother rabbit was broken into three small pieces.

I admired the pieces as I caressed them. What would the handi-craftsman think if he knew his artwork arrived damaged? I held the three pieces of the mother rabbit together. Perhaps I could glue them. Broken or unbroken, they deserved a magical story.

A disturbing crash outside jarred me back to reality. I took the fragile pieces and placed them back in the egg, tucking the ceramic gift in my dress pocket. Then I headed into the dining room to peer out the window.

The white dog I saw a few days earlier stood outside our apartment. Should I go out or would she run away? What would I do if she came up to me? I didn't have any dog food.

The dog's brown eyes tugged at my heart. She wagged her tail once she saw me in the window. Hope covered her face. She lifted her ears as if waiting to hear the door open. Did I have the heart to disappoint her?

Nobody in the apartments could have dogs. They weren't allowed —stupid apartment rules.

Reluctantly, I turned from the window and sat at the table again. I banged my fist and shoved the pencil off the table. It fell onto the floor and rolled away.

"I hate you, God—you hear that? You send me broken toys and take away my best friend, give me parents who don't understand me and teachers that hate me. That's fine. I can take it. Then you tease me with a dog I can't have."

The bare walls were silent, and I buried my face in my arms and sobbed.

I couldn't cry all afternoon. I went into the bathroom and grabbed some toilet paper to blow my nose. I didn't feel like writing. The last time I wrote something, my teacher accused me of plagiarism. Maybe I could do math. Whoever discovered Algebra must have been a fiend— how else could something so awful be invented?

I reached into my backpack for my library book, *The Diary of Anne Frank*. I was about halfway through it and identified with Anne's feelings of isolation. "Great," I mumbled, when I found only textbooks. I'd left it at school, the one book I wanted to read.

The dog barked again. I stood and pressed my nose against the windowpane. The sun had dropped behind the trees, and she stood in the shadows wagging her tail. With her rear end stuck up and paws dug into the ground, she begged. "Come play with me."

I couldn't resist. I went to the door and stepped outside in the cold January air—just in time to see her run towards the back of the apartments. "No, come back," I pleaded.

The dog skirted the apartment building with a noticeable limp, dodging two dirty bikes and a rickety wagon. Then she passed two utility sheds before she reached the boundary of the apartments and blended into the woods. I hesitated. Did I want to chase her into the thicket? The sun was low, and twilight would soon bring nightfall.

She reappeared briefly, shaking as if fearful that I might follow her. Then I lost her in the shadows and was ready to give up when I saw her once again. My weak ankle slowed me down. I stared at the naked trees—the one place around here I didn't like in the winter. Then the dog reappeared not more than ten feet away.

"Wait," I called. "Please." As I stepped forward, I tripped over a hole. I fell sideways into a pile of decaying leaves that covered the forest floor, twisting my ankle. Beneath the leaves, a rock protruded, and my head smashed against the corner. Sprawled out on the cold ground, I was temporarily stunned. Did I break the egg? I grabbed the pocket where I had put it, but it seemed to be okay.

The dog stayed nearby, although at a safe distance. She reminded me once again of Much-Afraid from the donkey story. The resemblance was surreal. The dog crouched and edged towards me, her tail swishing the ground clean. She yelped as if she expected me to follow.

Lightly at first, vibrations thumped the ground like drumbeats. An airy breeze, much too warm for January, carried panpipe notes from afar and rustled the dead leaves underneath me. As I watched, they turned from crusted yellows and reds to bright green.

Much-Afraid, as I called her, whimpered. The dog raised her head, and her eyes searched the red sky. She stood on her hind legs, pumped her front paws, and sniffed frantically. Naked tree branches rustled in the breeze, and Christmas lights blazed through the barren canopy. Winter rolled back as a scroll and invigorated my dulled senses. Mesmerized, I entered a dreamy reality, as if I were in a theater waiting for the start of a long-anticipated movie.

The scattered leaves lifted in a circular motion. Three white doves floated down and tiptoed around me. Forget-me-not flowers sprang up along with purple, red, gold, and green blossoms. A sweet healing balm saturated the air. The doves cooed as they gathered around my ankle, soothing my injury, as a mother would caress a child. Then they kissed the wound on my head. Bands of light scattered in pulsating rings. After a few tantalizing moments, the birds flew away.

Blue neon lights accented by flowers led to an open door surrounded by gleaming diamonds. Could I walk that far?

"Shale, are you okay?" a female voice asked.

Who called my name? I looked up, but the light from above was too bright, although the gentle warmth comforted me. I only saw flowers.

I called out to the dog. "Much-Afraid?" I didn't expect her to appear, but I had the feeling I wasn't alone.

The bright light captivated me, but the cone was fading, and soon the beam would vanish. Blue lights along the walkway grew brighter leading towards an open door.

"Much-Afraid?" The silhouette of a dog covered the opening briefly. She sat waiting.

"Much-Afraid."

"Follow me," a female voice said.

Was that Much-Afraid speaking to me? The effervescent light from the doorway bubbled in multi-colors. I stood and tested my ankle. As I tiptoed along the walkway, too afraid to believe I could run, light bubbles floated by as the diamond archway grew brighter.

The dog became visible once more.

"Shale," the voice called again.

"Wait! I want to go with you." Without hesitating, I stepped through the open door. I reached for her as she slipped through my fingers. Then she was gone.

CHAPTER 5

T HE GARDEN

The portal opened. A kaleidoscope of soft lights floated around me, humming like musical snowflakes. Each was unique and lifted my spirits, making me long for something I couldn't quite touch. An image came to me of a quiet, secluded park where one might go with a best friend. The experience lasted until the musical snowflakes turned to bubbles and then dissipated. The soft mist lifted, revealing a display of endless flowers that covered everything.

The view in the woods was a glimpse of the garden that now spread in all directions. Greens, blues, reds, purples, oranges, and colors I didn't have a name for covered the ground. The place looked like Oz. Maybe the Munchkins were hiding. All I needed was Toto— or a charming prince to kiss me so I would turn into a princess. Then I'd live happily ever after—except I wasn't ready to get married—or maybe it was a frog I was supposed to kiss.

Where was I? The doorway had disappeared, but I noted it was near an alcove of diamonds. Colorful flowers covered the embankment. The rock I tripped over while chasing the dog mysteriously glowed. The sizzling letters carved into the surface spelled e-b-e-n-e-z-e-r.

"Much-Afraid!" I called her several times. I heard a female voice, but was it the dog speaking to me?

The grassy knoll was like a carpet in front of the hidden doorway. Surrounding the knoll were ribbons of more multi-colored, sun-loving plants—lavender catmint, zinnias and roses. Black-eyed Susan's basked in the sun on the adjacent rolling hillside.

Along the pathway, crystal rocks, accented by clusters of smaller blooms, created a labyrinth of color and texture with alternating flowers and crystals. The large formations reflected the delicate blossoms where butterflies danced. The crystals seemed alive.

I squatted down to examine one. A distorted image emerged on the face of the crystal. I waited to see if it would materialize completely. Winged creatures flying around in a dark cave came into focus. Then I saw the white dog. Heavy ropes bound me as I sat on a rock slate. "No!" I cried—and the image dissolved. I staggered back from the rock and shook my head to erase the disturbing vision. What had seemed so perfect until now apparently wasn't. I would stay away from the crystals.

I followed the trail lined with flowers. The double and triple blooming roses were striking—without the rust the flowers had in our yard. Other plants were more exotic looking. I couldn't identify them.

As I strolled along, rose heads followed me like gyroscopes. When I stopped moving, they stopped. I reached over to pick one of the red blooms. As I bent the stem, a snake slithered though my fingers. I screeched and yanked back my hand. When I examined my fingers, they looked normal—no bite wounds, redness, or indication that something had touched me, but I could still feel the soft skin of a snake. The stem was indented where I had bent it.

Worry crept into my heart. Who brought me here and why? Was anyone watching?

I headed back to the grassy knoll spooked. I didn't want to follow the path anymore, but distant voices from farther along the trail now piqued my curiosity. The voices came and went, rising and falling, though not loudly enough for me to hear what they were saying. Child-like laughter followed a deep male voice. Although I worried about what I might find, I couldn't resist checking them out.

I walked several yards farther. Around a bend in the path, a long stairway was carved in the rocks. At the bottom lay Fifi. My heart skipped a beat, and a hot flash swept over me. Who was doing this? Why would I see that here?

As I stepped forward, the stairway faded. A descending path lined with more flowers sprouted up on both sides. I rubbed my eyes that seemed to be playing tricks on me. Did I want to keep going or head back? The doorway had vanished. Panic gripped me—whether I stayed or went back. Paralysis of thought swept through my emotions.

"Who's there?" My voice seemed small and insignificant in the garden.

The trail opened to a large grove of apple trees. Unexpectedly, I spotted a large, gray donkey and a small white rabbit lounging under a tree. The donkey was warming himself on a brown blanket, staring up at the sky with his legs crossed. The rabbit, wearing a blue bonnet with white flowers poking out the top, sat perched on a rock. They looked like friends on a leisurely picnic.

I crept closer sneaking behind some blueberry bushes. The plump gray donkey with extra-long eyelashes had a brown knapsack beside him. He stuck his head into the bag and rummaged. The bunny jumped off the rock and onto the blanket. I gawked at the animals.

The fresh aroma of apples and blueberry aroused my appetite. I tasted a blueberry, but it was sour, so I spit it out.

The donkey pulled out a bright red apple and chomped down. "Yummy." He rolled his eyes. "But I only have three left."

The rabbit licked her fur and wiggled her nose. "You and your apples. Don't you get tired of eating them?"

He took another bite. "Do you get tired of cleaning yourself?"

"Humph! Why would I get tired of that? I like to be pure white."

"I feel like that about apples."

"You like them to be pure white, too?"

The donkey twitched his tail. "No, that's not what I mean. I mean I like to eat them."

"How many donkeys eat apples?"

"How many have you met?"

The rabbit squinted. She held up her front paw as if indicating one —"Oh, my, a tiny speck of dirt." She went back to her scrubbing.

The donkey burped. "Maybe I should save the rest for tomorrow." He inspected the knapsack and twitched his ears. "I can't wait." He took one more and closed his eyes.

"Cool," I said, under my breath, giggling quietly—a fat donkey and a silly, talking rabbit.

The pleasant sound of trickling water reached me, and I fell under its spell. I had forgotten about the strange apparitions when out of nowhere a gryphon—half-eagle and half-lion—sky-bombed me. The creature came within inches of my face, lunging at my eyes.

"Help me!" Falling forwards, I anticipated talon-like claws hooking into my back or head. Why had I worn a dress? I buried my face into my arms and waited, huddled in a ball, too terrified to look up. Nothing happened. When I peeked out, I didn't see anything but a surprised donkey and startled rabbit staring at me.

Their curious looks miffed me. They could have done something to scare the creature away. I fumbled for words as I tried to catch my breath.

"A strange-looking bird attacked me. It came from that direction. Did you see it?"

The donkey shook his head. "Did you see anything?"

The rabbit laughed. "I saw an animal with two legs that rolled along the ground that scared the bejeebers out of me."

"Humph." I gawked at the rabbit who had insulted me. "You had to have seen it," I exclaimed. "It was large, and part of it had legs like a beast and—he almost poked my eyes out. I pointed to the blueberry bushes where a white dove was preening. "He was in my face. Over there."

The donkey finished chomping on another apple. "Who are you?

"How is it you can talk? Donkeys can't talk."

The donkey strolled up close to me, almost touching my face with his nostrils.

I slapped him across the nose. "How rude." I jumped back. "You're a smelly donkey at that."

"I don't smell," the donkey retorted. "And, fortunately, you don't either."

"Of course I don't smell."

"I wanted to see if you smelled like an underling. Besides, you're too pretty. You must be a princess."

I wiped my face, even though he hadn't actually touched me. "You need to mind your manners."

"*Heehaw*. Who is the visitor here, you or me?"

What was the point of arguing? "Whatever."

"You don't smell like an underling. You must be a princess," the donkey insisted.

I scoffed. "A princess? What do you know about princesses?"

"If you're going to insult me, you can go someplace else."

I glared at the donkey that seemed to be doing his best to irritate me. I stomped my foot. "I didn't like you being so close to me—and I sure don't like being smelled. It's insulting."

"I wanted to sniff you—to see if you had that stench on you."

"I don't smell."

"But the underlings do," retorted the donkey.

"What are you talking about?"

The rabbit wiggled her nose. "You aren't as pretty when you have a scowl on your face."

"What?" I touched my face as her words sunk in. How could a rabbit make me feel so irritable?

"I'm not angry," I shouted.

The two of them exchanged glances. "Are you sure she's not an underling in disguise?" the rabbit asked.

"An underling? What's that? And where in the universe am I?"

The donkey shook himself—like a dog shaking off water— arched his neck, and held his head high. He spoke like an orator. "You're in the king's garden, where it's always light and never dark—except when the underlings sneak in and steal what doesn't belong to them. Beyond the river and the forest is the king's palace—a mansion on the mountain where you're always welcomed. Never a stranger has visited the king."

"Are you a princess?" the rabbit asked.

"I'm no princess, although I wish I was."

The gullible creatures displayed an innocence that was disarming. Where on the planet did talking animals exist? Surely, Disney would have discovered them.

"What are you doing here?" the donkey asked.

My anger had melted so I told them my strange story, ending with the elusive dog. "She disappeared in an invisible doorway, and I can't find her."

The donkey's eyes got wide. "A doorway? I came through a gate guarded by an angel with a flaming sword. I was afraid, but the king called my name."

"Someone called my name, too."

"I hope you find your dog, little lady. I haven't seen one in the garden. We have a brown puppy that comes around to play with Cherios."

"My name is Shale," I corrected. "Not little lady."

"Pardon me, but you seem bossy for a girl."

I glared at him. "Don't donkeys say something like heehaw? I'd like you better if you were a normal donkey."

"I am normal. I have a larger vocabulary than heehaw."

How could an obstinate, fat donkey with extra-long eyelashes get me so upset? "You're rude, in case you didn't know it."

The donkey softened his words. "I once had a friend like your dog —sweet and all white, back in the cave at the grand estate of my former master."

"And I bet your name is Baruch, huh?" I said sarcastically.

"Yes, that's the name the king gave me."

I shook my head. "I admit you look like that other donkey in the book—gray with a white belly, and a fat one at that—even the extra-long eyelashes. Of course, I've never met a donkey. Was the name of your friend Much-Afraid?"

Baruch's eyes lit up. "How did you know?"

The white bunny wiggled her nose. "Where did you say you're from? Most of the king's animals don't come to our part of the garden. You seem to know a lot about the king's animals."

"She's a girl," corrected Baruch. "Not an animal."

"Yes, that's what I mean. A pretty girl."

I did a slight curtsy. All the similarities to my favorite book when I was young seemed more than strange—an outlandish tale of fantasy and mystique. I shook my head—was I dreaming? There must be an explanation.

I put my hand on my chest. My heart was beating. I blew on my hand, and cool air hit my palm. I was alive. How could all of these strange things be happening?

The rabbit hopped up beside me holding a white flower in her mouth. She had pulled it off her bonnet.

I gently took the flower out of the rabbit's mouth. "Is this for me?"

"Your present," the rabbit said.

I blew on the blossom, and the petals, carried along by the breeze, floated away. I scratched her behind the ear. "Thank you."

"Cherios." She pointed to her white fluffy chest. "I'm a garden bunny."

I patted her head, and she planted a kiss on my cheek.

Baruch stomped his hind legs. "Why can she kiss you, and I can't even get close to you?"

"Because she's a cute rabbit."

Baruch showed his white teeth in a pretentious smile.

"Besides, you're a male—go find a female donkey."

Baruch hung his head apologetically. "I want you to like me."

"Well, I do like you. I just—I grew up in the city. I'm not used to being around donkeys."

Neither one of us said anything for a minute—we had gotten off to a bad start.

Baruch changed the subject. "Tell me more about that book with the donkey."

I shrugged. "One day I found it on my bookshelf. Mother never bought me books because we didn't have any money."

Baruch's lopsided ears perked up. "Keep going."

"You ran away—sort of like me—and met a powerful king."

"And—"

An imminent coughing attack tickled my throat. "I'm thirsty. Can we get some water? And then I'll tell you the rest."

We meandered through tropical ferns, shady plants, and water oaks with delicate moss gracing the branches. The winding trail opened up to a clearing that led to a sandy beach bordering a luminescent river. Water lilies floated in the middle where lazy turtles had fallen asleep on a log that stretched across to the other side. They plopped into the river as we approached. The ripples spread out to the water's edge and lapped the sandy beach. I peered at my reflection.

"What's wrong?" Baruch asked.

"Nothing, but my hair is a tangled mess." I lifted the long strands over my head and rolled them into a bun. Then I caught movement among the tree canopy. Several dozen crows had gathered—spooky-like because there were so many. I couldn't ignore their loud, irritating cackles.

Baruch squinted and blinked his long eyelashes several times. "The crows have returned."

"Oh, dear, oh, dear." Cherios hopped about in a circle, wringing her paws. "I don't like it when the crows return."

CHAPTER 6

B ANISHED FROM THE GARDEN

What could be so bad about a few cackling crows? And why did I wear a dress? I couldn't swim with it on, and I wasn't going to take it off. I glanced at Baruch—a talking, male donkey. So tempting, but no, I wasn't going to swim in my underclothes.

I slipped off my shoes and lifted up my dress above my knees. After tiptoeing to the water's edge, I stepped into the cool river. I waded out a few feet before the water came up to my knees. Golden rocks covered the river bottom and dazzled in the sun—like an enchanted pool. I started to pick up one, but then I remembered the flower stem that turned into a snake. My fear returned.

More crows gathered, but they had become quiet. Dozens sat in the trees. "Is that their rookery?" I asked.

Baruch shook his head. "We never have any crows here—except when we're invaded by the underlings."

I was enjoying the water too much to worry about underlings. After a few minutes, I got out and climbed up on a flat rock. As I lay on my stomach, I dangled my arms out over the edge of the river. A blue bird darted up and danced over the water.

"She's so cute," I said, fascinated by the small-winged creature.

"They are terrible," Baruch said. "Not the bird, I mean the underlings. Most of the time, they don't have real bodies, they shape shift, although they look similar to large black bats. The acrid stench always precedes their appearance. I smell them coming now."

"I don't smell anything," I said, absentmindedly.

Cherios nervously twitched her ear to one side. "I hear the cackling again."

Which was cuter, the bird or the bunny? The tiny creature moved its wings like a hummingbird, although it was slightly bigger. After a few minutes of graceful gyrations, the bird landed on my shoulder.

"I'm Nevaeh, and you are a daughter of the king," the winged animal whispered, and then he flew away.

Why did it tell me that?

I scooted forward. Cupping my hands, I gulped several sips of water.

The golden rocks glittered on the bottom and cast a golden reflection on the surface of the water, but the sun's rays immersed the river in a shimmering white light. I reached down and picked up one of the nuggets. I gently turned it over in my hand. "If I didn't know any better, I'd say this is gold."

"Take as many as you want," Baruch said. "But hurry."

The trees creaked as the wind picked up. Overhead, more crows circled.

Baruch turned. "We better hurry to find cover. I smell the underlings."

I slid off the rock and tried to put the golden nugget in my pocket, but the egg was in the way. I set the rock on the grass. When I pulled out the egg, I opened it to make sure the bunnies were still there.

Cherios hopped over to look. "Oh, they are so cute. It must have been a very unusual chicken to lay that egg."

I laughed. "It's not real. I just wish the rabbits inside weren't broken."

Cherios nudged closer to me to see. "I didn't know chickens have bunnies in their eggs."

"No, you've got it all wrong. The artist sculptured the egg to hold the bunnies inside."

Cherios still looked baffled. "If you ever decide you don't want the egg and the rabbits, will you give them to me?"

I nodded.

Baruch brought over another nugget in his mouth and plopped it on the ground. "You can put that in my knapsack, and you might want that white pearl. Then we must leave the area as that is the underlings' entrance to the garden."

The knapsack was too full with Baruch's apples, so I didn't pick up any more. What a shame to leave them if they were worth something.

Where was I, talking to prissy rabbits and bossy donkeys? Unbeknownst to me, the dark magic grew. Floating over the river, an ominous cloud approached. When I turned and saw it, fear swept over me. A misty fog seeped from the pea soup and overflowed the river's banks. The garden shimmied and quaked, and the mist spread in all directions.

Soon lightning bolts struck the ground. The bolts splintered the trees, and limbs fell around us. My eyes burned from the acrid smell, and I grabbed Baruch's mane and covered my face. The sweeping murkiness was like a glove that groped everything in its path.

Shadows crept into the hidden pockets and tiny crannies, and scampering animals rustled through the leaves. The garden became quiet. Suddenly Baruch leapfrogged over a clump of rocks, knocking me backwards.

"Wait," I cried. Baruch paid me no attention. I shouted louder. "I want to go back. Get my shoes."

Baruch scowled. "You get them yourself."

Me? I bolted over to grab them. Seeing Baruch's knapsack, I scooped it up along with the blanket. I ran back and dumped everything beside the panicked animal.

Cherios panted heavily as she hopped over to catch up. "Baruch, you're stepping on me," she said shrilly.

"You're under me," Baruch complained.

"I'm hiding," she said, as if under his belly was a good place to hide.

I wanted to put Cherios on Baruch's back, but I needed to drape the blanket on him first. I slipped on my shoes—yuck. Wet sand coated them.

I couldn't stop shaking, although I wasn't sure if it was because I was cold or because I was scared. Fighting the wind, I got the blanket to stay on Baruch's back long enough to put Cherios on it, but when I went to pick her up, I couldn't find her. Where did she go?

The howling wind knocked more limbs to the ground. I climbed on Baruch's back. "Take me to the door, I want to go home."

"Grab my knapsack," Baruch said, "and hold it for me."

"I don't care about your knapsack. Let's go."

"Not without my apples."

"We're going to die—go." The stubborn donkey wouldn't move. I slid down and grabbed the bag, which seemed unusually heavy. "What do you have in this thing?"

Baruch stomped his hindquarters. "*Hee-haw*. Hurry."

"All right. I am." I tied the knapsack around his neck and hopped back up. The wet blanket was cold underneath me.

"Don't fall off," Baruch shouted.

"Do you see Cherios anywhere?" Then I saw her bonnet flattened in the wet sand. My heart sank.

A rancid odor turned my stomach, and I started breathing through my mouth. We wouldn't make it back if we stayed to hunt her down.

Every living thing had vanished. Some headed into the woods— maybe they knew a shortcut— others took the path as we did to the grassy knoll.

"Cherios?" I called. Perhaps she hadn't waited for us.

Baruch bolted up the trail as I struggled to keep from falling. I had never ridden on a donkey, and it was nothing like a horse. Not that I had ridden on a horse either, except at a camp with a handler walking beside me.

I glanced back and saw the mysterious cloud from the river following us—chasing us from the king's garden. The blob was thick and impenetrable, and it acted as if it were alive. No ordinary cloud, the pursuit left me breathless and terrified.

As we neared the grassy knoll, the door of escape reappeared. A vortex of swirling, distorted images faded in and out. I searched for Cherios, but the shifting cloud crept closer.

"Baruch, what should we do?"

The donkey ignored me. I clung to his back as he leaped into the portal. The once magical garden faded behind us. We passed through shadows eclipsed by stars on a moonlit night, arriving at a garden unfamiliar to me but not to Baruch.

CHAPTER 7

S URPRISES

"I know this garden," Baruch said. "This is where I was taken by the sheep when the king called me."

A high rock wall enclosed the garden, and a clump of thick olive trees provided a false sense of security. The place was dark except for two fire pits cradling a fire by a stone entrance. The moving shadows in the fire reminded me of the cartoon characters on my bedroom walls —except these were more ominous because of their enormous size.

"Where are we?" I asked. "Besides an olive garden that looks familiar to you?"

"Shhhh. If the guard discovers us, we're dead."

"What guard? Come on, don't scare me." My hands were cold, and I stuck them under the blanket to keep them warm, but the wetness didn't help much.

Baruch lifted his head and flared his nostrils. "The smells are familiar, too."

"What smells?" I couldn't smell anything.

Across the way, lights flickered on a steep hill that sloped into the next valley. I wished I could see more. Baruch leaned forward and stretched out his head. His wide nose reached for familiar scents. "I smell people, fish, vegetables, and wine."

"People?"

"From the village. It's not far."

I still couldn't smell anything, but howling wolves made me uneasy. Baruch took a few steps forward to get a better view. Rustling leaves startled me. Baruch swung around in a circle, and two savage-looking eyes that glowed in the dark confronted us.

"Get us out of here!" I choked.

Baruch dug in his hoofs and bared his teeth. "I'm not a horse." Holding his head high, he uttered a loud bray.

The wolf snarled, arched its tail, and pulled its ears back to challenge him.

"You're going to get us both killed," I whispered.

He growled and assumed a crouched position as if to lunge at us.

"Baruch, back off," I pleaded. "I don't want to die."

"If I run, he'll crush my neck."

Nevertheless, Baruch edged away, a few inches at first, and then a few feet. The wolf dropped its arched tail, but still showed its large canine teeth. The animal curled its mouth into a sinister smile.

"Baruch, make a run for it now. You've got a chance."

Without warning, Baruch heehawed and bolted, snapping off branches and slapping leaves in my face. I grabbed him around the scruff of the neck He tore through the trees, catching his knapsack on a limb. I reached out to save it.

The olive trees looked like shaggy ghosts in the moonlight and waved sinewy fists. I buried my face in Baruch's neck. Suddenly, he panicked, running around aimlessly in circles. This must be the end. I remembered my family and a report I once cheated on. Would anyone ever find me?

A loud yelp pierced the thick darkness. Baruch stopped. I held my breath, fearing the wolf would charge us again. A sudden jarring movement and rustling of branches disturbed the silence. In a hysteric frenzy, the wolf jumped out of the thick underbrush, his long body silhouetted in the moonlight. He was no longer chasing us—he was running away from something, but what?

Something moved behind us. The swishing noise cut like a knife at my heart. I muffled my screams in my hand and clenched my eyes. I was too terrified to look. Whatever it was, it was trailing us.

Baruch ducked behind an olive tree, and I slid off his back. I'd had enough. A man, dressed in a long drab-colored robe, strode past. In the dim light, he seemed to be holding something similar to a sling. I dared not move, lest he see us.

Could he be the gardener or night watchman? Whoever he was, he saved us from the savage wolf.

We waited a while longer, too afraid to make a sound.

The silence was broken by Baruch. "Shale."

"What?"

"Something is kicking me on the side."

I peered through the darkness. "What did you say?" I tiptoed towards him, ready to flee if something lunged at me. Baruch's plump body reflected in the moonlight with his knapsack hanging on his shoulder. "There's nothing near you. I can't see anything."

"There it is again. I felt something."

I moved the branches around and examined his protruding belly. "Felt what? There's nothing here. You're frightened, imagining things."

"No, it's still doing it. I tell you, I feel something on my side. Is it coming from my knapsack?"

"Your knapsack?" I glanced at Baruch's side and my heart pitter-pattered. "Baruch, there's something alive in your knapsack. What did you put in it?"

Baruch flailed his head around and stomped his hoofs. "Get it off me."

"Not so loud," Struggling with the cord in the dark, I tore it loose and dumped it on the ground. The knapsack landed hard with a thump. Bulging left, right, up, and down, at last, the top flung open. Something white popped up in a blur. Startled, I fell back into some thorny briars and the spiny branches held me like a spider.

"It's Cherios. What are you doing in there?" I exclaimed.

"I hid. It was too tight so I ate an apple." Cherios threw the apple core onto the ground. "Uh, where are we? This isn't the king's garden."

Sharp barbs dug into my side. I didn't move. "Welcome to Planet Earth."

Cherios scrunched up her nose as if she didn't understand.

"Seriously, we went through a gate, a doorway into another place. I don't know where we are."

Cherios's eyes bulged. "Can't we go back to the king's garden?"

Baruch twitched his tail. "You want to go back and be pursued by that dark shape shifter that was chasing us?"

Cherios held up her paw and examined it. "It's dirty here. I don't like this place."

In the moonlight, Baruch saw his eaten apple lying on the ground.

"You did eat my apple."

"It was tasty. I couldn't fit in the knapsack otherwise." Cherios looked sheepishly at Baruch. "Are you mad at me?"

Baruch rolled his eyes. "You scared the bejeepers out of me, that's all."

"Can't you get us back?" Cherios asked. "You got us here. You must know the way."

"I don't know how we got here," Baruch said.

"Oh, dear me, what shall we do?"

"We're going to go back home—my home—as soon as it's light enough," Baruch said.

"Do they have carrots?"

"I guess so."

Cherios licked her front paw.

The briars entangled me, and I couldn't move without scratching my arms and legs. Suddenly Cherios hopped away.

"Come back here," I shouted.

"Not so loud," Baruch said.

"Go get her. I can't move in these thorns. Why did she take off anyway?"

Baruch swished his tail. "I think she panicked."

"Go get her and come back. Don't leave me here."

While Baruch chased down Cherios, I climbed out of the thistles enduring scratches on my arms and legs. Why would there be so many thorns in a garden? And why did I wear a dress?

The night air was chilly, and with the adrenaline wearing off, I was cold. I crossed my arms and rubbed them to generate warmth. A few minutes later, Baruch returned, carrying Cherios in his mouth. He plopped her down, and I grabbed her by the scruff.

"Are you okay?"

She nodded, wide-eyed.

"You can't go running off like that. There's a wolf around and a night watchman. We aren't in the king's garden anymore. It's dangerous. You hear?"

Cherios nodded again, but didn't say anything.

"Baruch, we need a plan." I took the blanket off his back and plopped Cherios down in its place, and then put the blanket on top of her.

"Why did you do that?" Cherios asked.

"So you can't run off. We don't want you having panic attacks."

Cherios fidgeted underneath the blanket, but seemed resigned to stay put. Fatigue came over me. Morning was setting in, and we hadn't slept.

"I saw the entrance over there," Baruch said. "It's about a two-day walk from here to my master's estate."

"Estate? That sounded impressive, although I didn't want to walk for two days to get there. I was hungry, tired, and wanted a shower.

I scrunched my dirty dress where it was torn and picked off a briar. "We need food, and I need more clothes. Where are we going to sleep?"

Baruch nudged his knapsack still on the ground. "Are the rocks in there?"

"What? Oh, yeah, the golden rocks." I dug into the knapsack to see how many we had. "We have one apple, the white pearl, and one golden nugget." Why hadn't I grabbed more? Dozens covered the bottom of the river. I found one more in my dress pocket.

"Baruch, we could sell this pearl."

"Yeah, we'll try in the village."

After a short while, we found the opening to the garden. We took the dusty road leading away that disappeared into a secluded valley before climbing up the other side of the mountain. Fiery beams of light splashed over the crusty hills in the early morning. Here and there, sego palms and low-growing plants found water and clung to the rocky terrain. Sheep and goats wandered about in a field guarded by a young shepherd with a bony staff. The road stretched forever in snaky turns and sharp twists along the mountain passes. A strong gust of wind blew sand in my eyes.

"How much longer?" Cherios asked from underneath the blanket.

My parched throat and rumbling stomach made me irritable. "I don't know."

Buzzards flew by as if looking for carrion, and a band of wild camels stirred up a dust storm in the distance. I did a double take. Where were we? After several hours, the sun climbed overhead and burned us. Our pace slowed from fatigue. How many people died in the desert for lack of water? Some travelers passed us on the road. We were getting close to civilization.

"Where are we?" I asked the donkey. My lips felt swollen, and my rear end was sore from sitting so long on a bony animal. The men wore togas and looked poorer than a penny stuck in a gutter. They also stank. Did anybody around here bathe?

"We're getting closer," Baruch said. "Everything looks the same as before."

The little hump on Baruch's back bobbed up and down. "I'm tired of being trapped under this blanket," Cherios whined. "I can't see anything. Plus I'm hot."

"We're almost there. Wait."

The sun clipped the precipice of the jagged mountains in the distance, its rays casting shades of pink over the desert landscape. I missed home—my forest green bedroom that Mother said I could repaint ocean blue, my collection of fantasy books, and my best friend, Rachel. All I could think about was Atlanta.

Deep down, I had longed to run away but this was not what I had in mind. If I ever found that white dog, would she be able to lead me home? How would anybody find me here? Was this God's way of getting back at me—giving me a taste of the king's garden and then taking it away to punish me?

I wiped the sweat off my brow with the back of my hand, and more drops beaded up. My torn and dirty clothes disgusted me, but Cherios's wails under the blanket kept me from wallowing in self-pity.

"Baruch, let's stop for a second." I lifted the blanket off her sullen face. Her glossy eyes were sad.

"I don't belong here," she confessed. "I was just so afraid, I wanted to hide. Oh, what have I done, what have I done?" She sobbed.

Baruch's ears stood on end. "I hear horses. We'd better hide."

I lowered the blanket over Cherios, and we hurried behind a large boulder. Baruch stooped down, and I hid behind him. He shook violently. My heart thumped—if Baruch was scared, what did that mean for the three of us? The hoof beats approached. I tried to count how many riders there were. As they neared, they slowed down.

"Why are they stopping?" I asked Baruch.

"Shut up."

Cherios whimpered, and I whispered to her, "Be quiet."

"Whose voices are those?" she asked.

"Shut up, both of you," Baruch demanded. "Many robberies happen in the wilderness so you don't want to be seen. It's dangerous on the open roads."

CHAPTER 8

HERE AM I

The travelers stopped about fifty furlongs away in a clearing beside a rocky wall. They wore impressive headpieces that covered their faces, what soldiers wore during barbarian times, or so I remembered from *Gladiator*. Swords tucked into sheaths gleamed in the sunlight.

The men galloped across the desert when they were far away. Now that they were near us, they tarried, much to my annoyance.

One of the men slid off his horse and glanced in our direction. I pulled back out of sight. Baruch's heart thumped wildly against my cheek. The other riders pulled up and parked alongside the first man. What were they waiting for?

The first one dismounted and walked behind the rock wall. Metallic clanging rifled through the air as his armor came into view. A few minutes later, he reappeared stretching his back.

The man mounted his horse, waved at his comrades, and they took off, passing too close to our hiding place for comfort, but the galloping horses brought relief. The dust from the horses' hoofs filled the area. I began sneezing.

"That must be a record," Baruch said.

"Once I sneezed nineteen times."

Baruch rolled his eyes.

"Yuck. I'm so dirty," Cherios complained.

"You can clean yourself later," I promised.

The soldiers faded in the distance. We had escaped trouble this time. How would I have explained a stubborn donkey, a sweet bunny, and a fourteen-year-old runaway girl?

"Let's hope we don't see any more of those soldiers," Baruch said.

I lifted the blanket off Cherios and patted her reassuringly. "Just take us where we're going, Baruch. Thank goodness you know."

Never had I thought I would be indebted to a fat donkey. I stroked Cherios on the head. "You won't hop off now if I remove this, will you?"

Cherios sat scrunched up in a tiny ball on Baruch's back.

"You won't run away again, will you?"

"No."

I kissed her on the nose.

We continued along the narrow winding road through corkscrew mountain passes and a rocky desert wilderness. Before dusk, we arrived at a small village. The congested roads were crowded with travelers and merchants. Nostalgia swept over me as I saw young mothers with babies wrapped in their arms. The hordes of people slowed us down but also helped to conceal my strange clothing and fair skin. School-age children skipped past us with little more than a glance. I almost felt at home listening to their friendly chatter.

A plethora of smells—enticing, repulsive and raw—filled the dusty air from the road. Animal dung was the most revolting. I caught a young man staring at me. I told Baruch to push ahead. We came to a merchant with a scale similar to those in grocery stores.

We approached the trader and watched as he doled out three silver pieces to a man in front of us. "Let's check out that table, Baruch."

The shopper counted the money and recounted. "This isn't the right amount," he said. "You're cheating me."

The merchant crossed his arms. "What do you mean, this isn't the right amount?"

The disgruntled voices alarmed me. "Maybe we'll have better luck somewhere else." I patted Baruch on the back to keep moving.

Many of the women wore head coverings. I could cover my head with the blanket, but I needed to keep Cherios hidden. I rubbed her on the head to reassure her.

We passed several tables laden with fruit, bread, and fish. Soon we came to a booth with an assortment of pearls, perfume, and expensive-looking cloth of many colors. A young woman in a purple dress and a white-laced shawl greeted me with a warm smile. I slid off Baruch and walked up to her display.

She pleasantly asked, "Can I help you? You look like visitors."

My short flowery dress with spaghetti straps stood out against the long flowing wardrobe of the women. I chuckled. "Yes."

I handed her the white pearl. "How much will you give me for this?"

Her eyes brightened. "Oh, so beautiful." She examined it and admired the pearl before handing it back. "I'll give you thirty-five pieces of silver."

I wasn't sure how much that was. I picked out a purple dress. "How much?"

"Five pieces of silver."

Even though I swore I'd never wear another dress, I needed to look as if I belonged here.

The merchant smiled as she waited for my decision.

Encouraged, I asked her, "Is there a place we could stay overnight? I also need to put up my donkey."

She nodded. "My brother has a small inn up the road. Look for Jacob's Lodging."

"Jacob's?"

"You're a stranger here, aren't you?"

I nodded.

"Most foreigners stay there when they come to seek treatment from Doctor Luke. The inn is on the corner two furlongs east of Via Corneli, over the hill. In fact, he arrived last night from Jerusalem, my brother told me. Hurry before all the rooms are taken."

I froze on the word "Jerusalem." Is that where I was? How was it I could understand everyone? Did they speak English, too?

"Is everything okay?" the woman asked.

Her question brought me back to reality. "I'll look for the inn at once," I assured her. "Thank you."

The woman double-checked my purchase for flaws. "You will have plenty of oats and water for your animal. Tell him Martha sent you."

"Thanks again. I appreciate it."

She smiled graciously and turned to another waiting customer.

I started counting the silver pieces and caught a crow eyeing me. I kept counting—thirty pieces. That should be enough to pay for a night's lodging and food. I put them all in Baruch's knapsack, except for the last one.

I examined one of the coins and was surprised to see the word "Caesar" engraved on it. I flipped the coin over, and etched on the other side was the name "Augustus.' Why would I have a coin bearing the name of a famous Roman emperor?

The people were dark, making me stick out like a marshmallow. Most of the men had thick beards and long hair. The women were more olive toned, reminding me of Rachel.

I purchased some fresh fruit and sweet bread.

We came to a blind beggar holding out a small box. "Have mercy on me, have mercy on the blind man."

Most of the people skirted to the other side in ambivalence. My heart prompted me to stop.

"Wait, Baruch," I whispered. "Let's go back."

I slid off the donkey and placed a silver coin in his box.

He grabbed my hand, squeezed it, and then let go. "Thank you. May you receive a blessing."

I climbed back on Baruch's back and coaxed him to keep moving.

"*Ca-ca*, Baruch, good to see you."

Baruch whinnied, happy to see his old friend. "Worldly Crow!"

The talking crow lighted on a discarded jug a few feet away. "*Ca-ca*. I knew you were making a terrible mistake leaving, but you didn't listen to me, the stubborn donkey that you are. So you're back, uh? Where have you been?"

"I've been living in the king's garden a long ways from here."

"You haven't been gone long enough to travel far."

Baruch's eyes opened wide. "I've been gone for months."

"No, you haven't, my friend." Worldly Crow flew closer, landing on top of a wooden post.

"That's the same crow that watched me count the coins, Baruch."

"He's my stable buddy, Worldly Crow."

"And who is the speaking human?" the crow asked.

"I'm Shale Snyder."

"And you talk to animals?" He cackled. "Did they teach you that in the garden?"

"Yes—well, no. I mean, I don't know." I noticed some onlookers staring at me. Cherios poked her head out from underneath the blanket. I quickly covered her, but Worldly Crow saw the rabbit and cackled again.

I remembered why I never liked crows at our backyard feeder. They were too annoying. "We'll stay here in town tonight and catch up with you tomorrow." I hoped he got the hint.

Worldly Crow took off, but not before stealing a fish from a nearby table. The merchant waved his hands to shoo him away as the stolen fish dangled from his beak.

"Good riddance," the merchant complained. "Don't come back here no more."

I followed Martha's directions and we found Jacob's Inn up the road. After tethering Baruch, I walked to the front portico. Three men lay stretched out on rolled-up mats. The sickest one groaned in a monotone voice. He stopped when I approached. Another man had painful-looking sores on his arms and legs. Bugs circled about his wounds as he swatted at them. I didn't realize I was staring until one of them returned my gaze. His vacant eyes haunted me. I turned away. A doctor walked over to tend to him, blocking the sick man from my view.

I entered the inn where an attendant greeted me warmly.

"Are you Jacob?" I asked.

"No, but I know where he is." He called across the marbled portico. "Jacob, a young lady is here to see you."

Jacob stopped sweeping the floor and came over. "You need a place to stay tonight?"

I explained how his sister had sent me. Soon, another man strolled over and offered to take Baruch to the stable.

"I'll take good care of your donkey, ma'am," he offered.

"Thank you, sir. Can you tell me where I can get some carrots?"

"Carrots?" he repeated.

"Yes, sir."

"I'll see to it you receive fresh fruit and vegetables, ma'am."

The man spoke to another helper. "The young lady wants carrots."

A short time later, a servant brought me a large bowl of fresh fruit and vegetables. I handed her a silver coin, and she thanked me, beaming from ear to ear.

When no one was looking, I wrapped Cherios up in the folds of my dress and took her with me into my private room. The accommodations were modest and sparkling clean. Freshly-cut flowers adorned the wooden table and I even had a chair. Three colorful, thick blankets draped the simple bed. Cherios curled up on the end. After setting a bowl of fresh carrots in front of her, she took each one and nibbled gingerly.

"I could get used to this place," she exclaimed between bites.

I was surprised at how quickly she'd adjusted after being so panicked in the garden.

"You might need to—I have a feeling we'll be here for a while."

Later, I slipped out to check on Baruch. The evening air was cool and the setting sun dimmed my inn room to shades of gray. I'd have to get used to not having electricity. I welcomed the nippiness after being so hot earlier. Baruch was already asleep in his stall, opening one dopey eye wide enough to acknowledge me before dozing off again. I patted him between his ears and walked back to my lodging.

As I padded across the shortcut between the stable and the inn, a rustling noise betrayed movement in the tall grass. The blades of grass shimmied like a stadium of fans jumping up and down. I was too tired to inspect it now, but my memory would recall it later.

Later, in my room, after eating bread and grapes, I poured some wine into a mug. Everyone drank here, so why not? I had never tasted it. I took a couple of sips and gagged. Yuck. I stared into my cup debating whether I wanted any more.

"Do you not like your drink?" Cherios asked.

"Not so much." I discarded the wine and gulped some water to get rid of the aftertaste. Soon my eyes became heavy, even though I didn't want to fall asleep. I had too many things to think about, but I succumbed to the thick blankets draped over me and fell into a deep sleep.

I was lying on the beach listening to the ocean when I looked up into the sky. A hole formed in the middle of the clouds. The clouds surrounding the hole floated into magical shapes. The first one was a rabbit. The second one was an angel. The third appeared to be a donkey. They slid across the sky and faded, and the hole gradually disappeared.

Then a woman appeared who had severe features—a pointed nose, long face, high cheekbones, and a crooked neck. Unlike the others, she glared at me from the clouds. She knew me, but I didn't know her. I wanted her to fade away, but she wouldn't. Feeling trapped in my dream, I awoke.

I sat up, disturbed. The light from the moon filtered in through the window and cast shadows over the bed. Cherios was sound asleep. Shadowy cartoon characters scaled the walls. I couldn't get the cloud-shaped woman out of my mind. Who was she?

CHAPTER 9

WOMAN IN THE CLOUDS

The next morning, an annoying rooster awoke me. How many times did he need to cock "cockle doodle do"? I put the strange dream behind me, not wanting to let fear overshadow my already anxious thoughts. I slipped on my new dress, washed my face, and combed my hair as best I could. Water does miracles when you have no brush. A delicious assortment of fresh fruit and bread filled my stomach.

I wanted to leave before the sun became unbearable and I had too much time to think. When I entered the stable, Worldly Crow sat on a wooden beam in the rafters. Groomed and fed, Baruch looked handsome, a good thing since I had no idea how to take care of a donkey.

After tipping the man a silver coin, I climbed on Baruch's back and hid Cherios in the folds of my dress. How comfortable I had become riding on a donkey. Even Cherios was happy after eating two meals of fresh carrots and greens.

The winding road led down a steep mountain into another valley and then back up another mountain. At least I was riding, but my backside was sore from sitting on the donkey. My aches and pains distracted me from worrying so much about where I was or how I'd get home. I could only think about one thing at a time, although my thoughts always returned to the dog. What happened to her?

With lunchtime approaching, Baruch announced, "We're almost there."

What would happen when we arrived? How would I introduce myself?

Worldly Crow had flown ahead. A short distance away, a rock-stucco home abutted up against the side of a hill with a cave in the back. The building was three levels high, if you counted the roof as the third floor, with stone stairs on the outside. Surrounding the house was a large open field where sheep and goats were grazing.

I wished I'd never left home. "Baruch, what's your master going to say when I show up on his doorstep?"

"Oh, I didn't think of that. Don't let him know you can talk to me."

As if I'd tell him. I uncovered Cherios and patted her on the head. She snuggled up to me as she sniffed the air.

We entered a courtyard surrounded by early blooming spring flowers. Baruch stopped in front of a small grouping of palm trees.

A handsome young man with curly black hair, tanned skin, and broad shoulders approached. His deep-set eyes seemed too intelligent for this place. "I'll take your donkey for you," he offered.

He lifted me off Baruch and set me on the ground. "I hope you enjoyed pleasant travels," he added.

"Yes." My legs were wobbly after sitting for so long on the animal.

The young man focused on me with much interest. "Your father has been expecting you."

"What? What did you say?"

He stopped short. "You've traveled a long ways?"

"Yes. But what did you say about my father?"

A thin, long-faced woman interrupted our conversation. Her nose looked like a pencil point. I nearly fainted as the cloud-woman approached, wearing a forced smile.

"How are you, Shale? Your father is expecting you. He'll soon return from Jerusalem. I'm his wife, Scylla."

She extended her hand.

I reached out in return. "Nice to meet you," I stammered. My father? I wasn't sure if I should ask any questions. Was this some kind of elaborate prank?

She gazed at Baruch. "We missed Baruch. Glad he's back." Her focus returned to me. "You needed transportation, your father said." Her eyes roamed my body as if I had contraband. If you don't need your bag, my servant can take it for you."

I glanced at the young man and then back to my supposed step-mother. Why didn't I ask more questions about my father?

I'd much prefer talking to the good-looking dude. "This is Cherios. Can you take care of her, too, sir?"

"Yes, ma'am," the servant said. "I'll take the rabbit and donkey and give them food and water. Can I take your bag?"

"Bag? Oh, yes. The knapsack—uh, I want to hold on to this. Thank you."

I patted Baruch on the nose. "See you in a bit, and you, too, Cherios." I rubbed the top of the rabbit's head. "Here is her blanket, if you would take that, also."

"Yes, ma'am." The young man put Cherios under his arm and guided Baruch around to the back of the wealthy estate. I watched them until they disappeared.

Standing before my father's wife seemed very strange. I'd imagined this day coming—but a long ways into the future. She stood as a statue with her hands stuck in her two front pockets. Her stone face made me uneasy.

"Follow me," she said.

Maybe I could run away in the middle of the night. They sent a donkey to fetch me? How could that be? I was chasing a dog and happened to meet a donkey along the way.

The door opened to an elaborate earthen house. Rushes woven together covered the flat roof. Off the main room, three small adjoining rooms abutted. Elaborate rugs covered the wooden floors and the stone-hewn walls reminded me of fancy fireplaces back home. Wooden beams supported the walls and outside stone stairs led to a second floor.

Luxurious accommodations varied widely, but this was quite stark by American standards. Soon a servant brought a bowl of water and washed my feet.

Scylla's icy eyes made me uneasy. I pretended not to notice how much she disliked me.

"Where'd your dress come from?"

"I bought it."

"Oh, so you have money?"

I nodded.

"Tell me about your journey."

"What do you want to know?"

"What grade are you in school?"

"Ninth."

"Can't get along with your mother and stepfather?"

What business was it of hers? I ignored her question. "When is my father going to be here?"

"Soon."

Not soon enough. What had my mother told her about me?

Scylla continued. "Your mother didn't tell us when you'd arrive. Your father is a high-ranking Roman dignitary and had important business that couldn't wait. Theophilus called him back to Jerusalem for a few days. He'll be here tomorrow."

"Tomorrow?"

"Or the next day."

After an awkward silence, I asked, "How did you know I was coming?"

"A messenger arrived last week with a letter. It was not my decision to let you stay. It was your father's." Her tight lips turned into a forced smile.

"I see."

"You've never met your father?"

"No. He left when I was a baby."

"So your mother says. Do you want to know the story?"

"What?"

"She ran off with you. The law was after her for reasons you wouldn't understand—serious issues about your future and a pre-arranged marriage she wouldn't honor."

I doubted her statement. "Mother never told me anything like that."

Her demeanor softened. "You must be tired and need to rest." As she sauntered towards the door, she paused. "Don't give me any trouble. Your father has put me in charge of you. I'll trust you until you give me reason to think otherwise." Then she disappeared into an adjoining room.

What was that supposed to mean? A kinder woman's voice interrupted my musings.

"Come here," she said, "and sit at the table." The young woman brought in a tray of food—fish, olives, pomegranates, and bread. My heart pondered everything as I nibbled. I wasn't hungry.

She smiled. "My name is Mari."

"Nice to meet you," I mumbled. I didn't feel like being pleasant.

"Can I take you to your room now?"

"Sure."

We walked outside and she escorted me up the steps. The handsome man who had taken Baruch and Cherios from me when I arrived was in the field. "What's that man's name?"

"Daniel. He arrived a few months ago to help with Nathan. Very kind, smart as a wolf, but—I shouldn't say."

I glanced back at Mari. "Shouldn't say what?"

Mari's eyes looked sad. "I can't let him get too close to me. He would know too much." Then she smiled, as if I was supposed to understand what she meant, or she supposed I knew more than I did. I shrugged off her comment and called to Daniel, waving my hand. "Thank you for taking care of my animals."

He did a slight bow and nodded. "Yes, ma'am."

After Mari left, I peered out the tiny window that faced the rolling green hills. Sheep grazed in the pasture. A short distance away, a door opened into the rocky hill where the animals were in a small cave. I'd check on Cherios and Baruch shortly.

I stepped back from the window and observed my new surroundings. A bed was in the corner with a small wooden table beside it, similar to my room at Jacob's Inn. A wooden vanity was on the opposite wall with some female toiletries—perfume, powder, and make-up of sorts. Two small, multi-colored rugs covered the wooden floor. There wasn't much else. I'd at least enjoy trying out the makeup.

I laid down for what I meant to be just a few minutes—I wanted to see how comfortable the bed was—but I drifted off to sleep. A familiar bark woke me a few hours later.

CHAPTER 10

THE MEETING

Where was I? Groggy and disoriented, I twisted and turned to force myself awake. When I remembered, I stood and ran to the window. The sun had dropped in the sky, and the shadows from the trees were long. Nighttime approached.

Then I saw her, dreamlike—the white dog. Her eyes danced, and her small body sashayed at the hope of seeing me at last.

"Sleepy head, wake up," she demanded, "and come down here at once. I traveled the universe to bring you here, and I shan't wait any longer."

I shoved open the door and ran out. I saw the white dog before everything turned black. I squinted. Fifi lay motionless at the bottom of the steps. I heaved into the stony wall, clasping my stomach, as if I were going to bowl over.

When I reopened my eyes, the white dog was prancing as if she had won Best in Show at Madison Square Garden. She bounded up the stairs and ran into my arms.

I scratched her ear as she wiggled in my lap. "You aren't going to run away this time, are you? Can you talk, too, or was that my imagination?"

"All animals talk. Most people don't have the gift of understanding what we say."

"How did I receive the gift?"

"The king is the giver."

"The king?"

"The sheep sent me to you," the white dog said.

I patted her on the head. "So many unexplained things go back to that children's story."

The dog stretched and cocked her head enjoying the rubdown.

I laughed. "Is your name Much-Afraid?"

"I was always afraid until the king healed me."

I wanted to hold her tightly for a long time. The white dog nuzzled her head in my lap, and the more I scratched her ear, the more her affection warmed my heart.

"Did you know that dog is God spelled backwards?" the white dog asked.

"No. How did you know that?"

"The king told me."

"I wish I could meet him someday."

"You will."

"Tell me more about this king."

"He's perfect."

"Then I better stay away from him."

The white dog shook her head. "No, you got it wrong. The king knows you aren't perfect—but since he created you, he knows everything about you."

"Created me? My parents did that. No matter—maybe the king will adopt me and make me a princess, and I won't even have to kiss a frog."

"You underestimate the king's power," the white dog replied.

"What about you? I'm here because of you. Where are we?"

"We're where the king brought you."

"Brought me?" I eyed the dog skeptically. "So the king sent you to me to bring me here, and he wants to make me his daughter, but I don't yet know my father. Sounds like a story I might write someday, and I wouldn't be accused of plagiarizing—it's too fantastical." I laughed. "I just made up a word."

"The king loves magical stories."

"Maybe I'll be lucky enough to hear one." I looked at the dog's foot. "How come you have a limp?

"I don't."

"I saw you limping back at the apartment—twice."

"I was imitating you."

"What are you, some kind of psychiatrist?" I had almost forgotten about Dr. Silverstein.

"How did you hurt your foot?" the dog asked.

I stiffened as my joy fled. "It's healed now."

The dog changed the subject before I lied. "Come. Let me show you around the stable."

"I'm going to name you Much-Afraid. You remind me of the dog from my favorite childhood story."

"A rose by any other name would smell as sweet."

"A dog that knows Shakespeare." I laughed. A king of stories and coincidences? Lost in thought, I entered the stable. The cave was roomy and dry for an enclosure full of donkeys, pigs, goats, and sheep, and even some animals that weren't invited. Two mice scurried underneath the table. Baruch was munching on oats when I walked over to his stall. "I'm so happy to see you—in such a short time you've become my favorite donkey."

"And how many donkeys have you ever met?"

I held up my fingers and counted—one.

We both laughed.

"I'm happy to see you, too, Miss Shale."

I grinned. "How is Daniel?"

Baruch's eyes beamed. "We've got plenty of oats, fresh water, and a clean stall. Daniel is kind. Different."

The way Baruch said it reminded me of Mari's words.

Cherios hopped on the ledge and bobbed up and down. "I have lots of carrots and veggies."

Much-Afraid barked excitedly. "Come meet Lowly." Much-Afraid led me to his stall. A cute little pig wagged his short tail as he bowed. "Th-thank you for bringing Baruch b-back to us."

"You're welcome." I examined the stony walls and high ceiling. The other animals in the stable nodded at me but remained quiet—except for the fiery donkey in the back stall. He was a large, red-haired ass with a cantankerous disposition. Banging his backside into the wall, he grumbled and kicked the doorframe with his hoofs.

"What's wrong with him?" I asked.

Baruch jerked his head towards the back and whinnied. "Daniel gave me his stall and put him in that one. He didn't like being moved."

I studied the disgruntled donkey as he gave me a sarcastic smile. I leaned over and whispered in Baruch's ear. "Stay away from that brute, okay? He gives me the creeps."

CHAPTER 11

S ILENCE OF DESTINY

Later that evening, at mealtime, Scylla introduced me to the rest of the family—Nathan, who was mute, from my father's second wife (he was on his fourth); Mari, the housekeeper; and a couple of slaves whose names I couldn't pronounce. The conversation focused on governmental matters for which I had no interest. When they mentioned my father, my ears perked up, but mostly it concerned his work in the province. I still didn't understand what he did, except he kept the peace.

I caught Nathan staring at me several times during the meal. I looked away feeling awkward. How do you connect with a person who can't speak? It was hard to believe he was my half-brother.

"Has he ever said anything?" I asked.

Scylla shook her head. "When Nathan gets agitated, we send for Daniel and he calms Nathan down."

What would it be like not to be able to talk? The poor boy had straight brown hair and green eyes, like me, but was much thicker boned and a little too plump. In contrast, I could barely gain a pound. Nathan was two years younger. A mild disposition gave him a child-like innocence.

Scylla ended the evening by telling me I had to contribute to the running of the household if I planned to stay with them. They would enroll me in school as soon as possible. I should have known I couldn't escape that.

"You see the well in the distance?"

I nodded.

"You will need to fill the bucket up first thing in the morning."

"Okay."

Scylla's eyes narrowed. "You haven't done much housework, have you?"

"Why do you say that?"

She grabbed my hand and stroked it. "You have soft hands."

I jerked it away from her. "I have chores," I snapped.

"Good. We'll see what a good worker you are." Scylla walked over and picked up a cup, poured some wine, and headed to her private quarters, disappearing behind a closed door. It would be my luck to have a father with such poor taste in women. I shook my head in disgust. "Thanks for the delicious meal, Mari."

She smiled back.

After saying good night to Nathan, I climbed up the stairs on the outside of the house. The stars shone brightly, and I searched for the Big Dipper. Where were those four lights?

A breeze blew that cooled me off, slowing down my gushing thoughts. The gentle air lifted my spirits, whispering sweet lullabies into my racked brain. Did they hold the secret to my future?

An owl sent love notes across the hills. "Hoo-hoo-hoo-hoo."

No iPhones, no computers, no cars, no iTunes, no Internet, and no TVs. Tomorrow I hoped for answers.

CHAPTER 12

S HALE AND THE YOUNG MAN AT THE WELL

"Peet-sah, peet-sah." I was surprised to hear a flycatcher high above in the tress. His familiar call reassured me some things didn't change. I grabbed the bucket hanging on the wooden post and started down the stony path to the well. The sun hung brightly in the sky casting sharp rays on the rolling hillside. Dew droplets glimmered on the blades of grass. A cool breeze blew and flapped my long hair against my shoulders and into my face.

I set the empty bucket down and noticed a weary man sitting on a stump. A shawl hung down over his face, covering his eyes. A donkey stood alongside him. I did a double take—the animal looked like that red brute in the cave the day before.

"Could you draw some water for my donkey?" the man asked. He never looked up, but sat hunched over. He was young, perhaps a teenager. He must have been up at dawn to be so tired.

I reached for the rope and hooked it on the bucket, then lowered the bucket down. After filling it, I trudged the water over, taking care not to slosh it around. It was quite heavy to tote. I didn't know fetching water could be so hard.

As I approached the young man, he lowered his shawl and smiled. Aghast, I dropped the bucket. The water spilled out, scaring the donkey. He took off in a scramble. The spilled water drenched the boy and spread out in a puddle on the ground.

"Why did you do that?" The familiar man wiped the water off his arms.

I stood frozen as if shot with a stun gun. How could he be here? Memories hijacked me—the curse he put on me two years ago, the attack in the hallway, shaming me with the worm, and all the things too numerous to mention. He'd made my life hell. I hated him. How dare he follow me here! I began to hyperventilate, feeling my way behind me with my hands.

"Don't come near me or I'll kill you."

He blinked twice and laughed. "You kill me?"

I backed up some more. "What are you doing here?"

"I live here."

"You liar." Now I knew Judd was insane.

"You've come back after all these years. Your mother is more honorable than I imagined."

"What are you talking about?" I kept backing up until I felt a person behind me. Surprised—I didn't remember seeing anyone nearby — I turned. "Daniel."

He eyed both of us. "What's going on?"

Judd stood, lifting the shawl over his head and mumbling a few unintelligible words. Then he took off after his donkey.

I searched his face in disbelief. "Where did you come from?"

"I'll explain later, once I know you better."

"What's that supposed to mean?"

Daniel's eyes glanced over at the fleeing figure.

"Why are you so afraid of him?"

"What do you mean?"

"What did he do to you?"

The direct nature of the question startled me. "I don't want to talk about it, but thanks for coming."

Daniel picked up my water bucket and filled it. "Come, let's go. We'll talk about it later, when you're calmer."

We walked back to the house in silence.

Could I trust Daniel? Something mysterious about him piqued my curiosity, but I couldn't place my finger on it.

"After you eat breakfast, come find me in the cave," he said, "if you want to talk."

I stood in the back portico watching him walk away. Who was he?

CHAPTER 13

S TRANGE COINCIDENCE

After breakfast, I sat on a hewn log in the back portico. The air was dry, making my eyes sting and nose itch. A full-fledged pity party consumed me. Would I ever enjoy meals here?

My almost teenage half-brother had the annoying habit of making embarrassing, unintelligible sounds while eating, and my stepmother handed me a long list of chores. I was glad to help out, but I didn't want to be treated like a slave. I picked up a rock and skipped it across the ground, watching it disappear beneath half-dead weeds. Maybe I should leave, except I wanted to meet my father.

"*Ca-ca.* What's got you down?"

I looked up and spotted Worldly Crow peering at me from a palm tree a few feet away. He flew over and lighted beside me. His dark blue feathers shone in the harsh sunlight while his bulging eyes fixated on Baruch's red apple. I wasn't going to give it to him. I'd pulled it out of the knapsack—the very last one.

Worldly Crow cocked his head coyly. "Don't want to talk about it?"

I gazed off in the distance. "It's not what I had expected. That's all. I don't even know what I want. I just know this isn't it."

Worldly Crow sat listening. "Your father is on the way."

I sat up straighter. "He is?"

"Yes. He should be here later today."

"How do you know?" I was reluctant to believe him.

"I fly everywhere keeping track of the news of the day. I saw him myself, traveling up from Jerusalem. He's a very important man in the government, gone more than he's here. Be happy that you get to see him at all."

"Tell me more about him."

Worldly Crow cackled. "He likes to drink, and he likes women."

Just what I wanted to hear. "What else?"

"*Ca-ca.* He has lots of money."

"What else? Has he ever mentioned me?"

"I overheard him say you were coming. I didn't know you existed."

I laughed demurely. "So my father kept me a secret all these years."

"Now, listen here, little girl," the crow admonished. "I don't want you to be disappointed, but he's a diplomat in the Roman government. He may not have time for you. He has to tend to matters of the state and make important decisions."

"More important than his daughter?"

Worldly Crow ruffled his feathers at my rebuff. "I say it as it is. Take it for what it's worth." He eyed my apple. "Are you going to eat it?"

"No. This is for Baruch. He loves apples. The red ones are his favorite."

The crow smacked his beak. "Oh. We don't have anything like that around here. Where did you get it?"

"The garden. Now you know. It's the last one he'll get for a long time. Unless you can tell me something else about my father, I'm going to give this to him now."

The crow closed his eyes poetically. "Scylla has been fussing over you coming. She's protective of him."

"What do you mean?"

Worldly Crow sneered. "Everybody knows she married him for his money. Your father is a brilliant man except when it comes to women —his downfall."

Then the crow disappeared into the hedge. Good riddance. When I entered the cave, Baruch was not in his usual pen. Instead, the brazen donkey I had seen with Judd greeted me. I was afraid to approach him.

"If you're looking for Baruch, he's in the back," the fiery red donkey said.

"Why?"

"Judd put him back there. This is my stall, not Baruch's."

I kicked the door to his stall and gave him a dirty look.

"What's your name?"

"Assassin."

His name stopped me cold.

"Where did you get the apple?" Assassin asked.

"It's Baruch's from the garden. The last one."

"So he likes apples?"

"Yes." I examined Assassin. To think of him being around Baruch frightened me. I didn't trust him or Judd.

"I'm back here." Baruch's words trailed from the back of the cave.

I followed his voice, and my favorite trio greeted me. Cherios jumped into my arms, almost knocking the apple out of my hand. I glanced back at Assassin as the other animals watched us. I handed Baruch his apple, along with the knapsack. "I'm sorry I haven't been able to mend it yet. This is the last apple."

I leaned over his stall door and whispered, "You should savor it and eat it s-l-o-w-l-y."

Baruch had other ideas. He chomped it down in seconds.

Then the front door opened, and Daniel walked in. After wiping his hands on a well-used cloth, he plopped down on the bench. "How was breakfast?"

"Fine, but I'm not happy Judd put Baruch in the small stall in the back. Aren't you in charge?"

"Oh, Shale, does it matter? Aren't you being picky?"

"What do you mean, picky?"

"Judd knows how to take care of the animals. It's not as if Baruch is being mistreated."

"Why are you siding with Judd?"

"I'm not. I took over the animal care when your father hired me. Judd refuses to accept that I replaced him, but it's not as if Baruch is being abused."

"I don't want Baruch in the back by himself. He might get lonely."

Daniel rubbed his eyes and squinted. "We can move him."

"Got something in your eye?"

"No, it's not that." He rubbed his eyes some more, and I stopped talking, waiting until he wasn't distracted. Unexpectedly, a round plastic object fell on the table. He picked it up and hid it in his hand.

"What's that?" I asked.

"Nothing."

"Is that a contact lens?"

"What?"

"The thing in your hand?"

"No."

I stared at him. Things didn't add up. I had been here long enough to know they didn't make contact lenses around here. "Where do you come from?"

Daniel's eyes bore into me. "How perceptive you are." He fidgeted for a minute as I waited for an answer.

Finally, Daniel asked, "How do you know what this is?"

I spread my palms out towards him, waiting for him to answer me.

"Why don't you tell me about yourself," Daniel suggested, although not convincingly.

"Me? Tell you what?" Flustered, I turned away. He was the one with the contact lens. I wasn't going to tell him anything.

Daniel stood and began to pace. He came up behind me and stopped. "I need to be able to trust you."

"You can trust me."

He walked over to the bench along the wall, near the door, and plopped down again.

"Wait a minute." I glanced at Assassin—I didn't want him to over-hear. "Can you put Assassin to pasture?"

"Assassin?" Daniel looked perplexed. "How did you know his name?"

"He told me," I blurted.

"The donkey told you?" Daniel asked.

My face grew hot. "Well, sort of."

Daniel raised his eyebrow. "I'll put Assassin outside. Wait here."

A few minutes later, he returned, leaving the door ajar.

"Don't you want to shut the door? Someone might hear us."

"There's no one else around." He sat beside me at the table. We both started talking at once. I laughed. Daniel's eyes reminded me of Rachel's.

"So you can talk to animals?" he asked.

Would I reveal my secret? "Yes, I can talk to the animals, and they can talk to me."

Daniel rubbed the back of his neck intrigued. "Have you always been able to talk to the animals?"

"No. Someone called my name. That was the first time."

Much-Afraid padded over and sat beside me.

I scratched her behind the ear. "The first voice I heard was hers—I'm pretty sure—before I was transported to the garden."

Daniel glanced at Much-Afraid. "What garden?"

"The king's garden."

He leaned on his elbow and seated his chin in his palm. "The king's garden? Why don't you tell me from where you come."

I laughed. "You really want to know?" I began from the beginning and explained about the garden and meeting Baruch and Cherios. I told him how we had ended up at my father's home. After I finished, Daniel seemed more engrossed in the images carved on the back of the cave wall.

I examined his face and reached for his hand. "You think I'm crazy, don't you? I need you to believe me."

"No, Shale, you're not crazy. If you were, I would know. I came from a psychiatric ward."

CHAPTER 14

D ANIEL CONNECTION

My heart fluttered. "What? Please tell me you aren't psycho." I had studied schizophrenia in biology class.

Daniel laughed. "Relax. I'm not going to hurt you." His eyes followed the structure of the cave as if he were looking for something hidden in a crag.

I scanned his face for clues. "Why don't you begin with telling me how you have contact lenses when they don't even have phones or T.V.'s or toilets that flush. What are you holding back? I told you my story, now you've got to tell me yours."

"First let me see if I can get this thing in," Daniel muttered. He stood and walked over to a trough of water.

The mystery of who he was attracted me to him. I brushed my hair away from my face with my hands and wiped the perspiration off my forehead.

A few minutes later, with the lens back in his eye, Daniel returned to the table. He studied me for a second, nervously tapping his fingers on the table. "I'm going to tell you a mystery," he began. "Are you okay with that?"

"Sure." I leaned forward admiring his beautiful blue eyes—or was it the contact lenses that made them blue?

"Your father will be here soon. Things aren't as they seem. I mean, you're confused, right?"

I nodded. "That's an understatement."

Daniel leaned against the wall and told his story. "I'm from Jerusalem. 2015."

"2015?" I interrupted.

Slight irritation flashed across his face. "Wait until I finish before you start asking questions."

"Sorry for interrupting."

"Did anyone ever say you're impatient?"

"I'm trying to put it all together."

"If I stop and answer your questions, I won't get through it."

"Okay," I replied reluctantly.

"It's 2015, but no more questions."

"I come from 2012."

Daniel's eyes widened. "2012—three years ago."

"You're three years into my future."

"Wow!" Daniel cleared his throat. "Let me finish telling you my story, and then we can talk about that."

I nodded.

"I was in my senior year of high school and wanted to be a doctor. Of course, we have to serve two years in the army, so I knew it would have to wait a while."

"I know about the mandatory time to serve in the army in Israel. Rachel told me."

Daniel raised his eyebrow. "I had some extra time after school and volunteered at a nursing care facility in Jerusalem. It was close to our home—I could ride my bike. I needed some volunteer experience for my application to medical school."

"In the nursing home I met a famous general, General Ezra Goren.

He was an older man, a brave leader and war hero. May 14, 1948, is the most important day in our history. The last British forces left and David Ben-Gurion declared the establishment of a Jewish state. All the major powers recognized us, including President Truman and Joseph Stalin, but the Arabs were unwilling to accept the Jews having a homeland. Within hours, the surrounding nations attacked us. General Goren obtained weapons from sympathetic nations and smuggled them into Israel, enabling us to withstand the onslaught."

Daniel stood and walked over to the water barrel again. He returned with a mug of water and took a few sips before continuing.

His voice was thick with a strong Israeli accent, yet he spoke in perfect English. His eyes burned with passion, alive with the determination and strong will I'd seen in photographs of great leaders.

Daniel continued. "I had the utmost respect for General Goren. He told me stories about the war, how God performed miracles as the Israelis fought back the Arabs. He said no one believed we could win."

Daniel exhaled.

Captivated, I listened. "I never knew about all of that."

"You'll learn about it when you take world history in high school."

"Sounds more interesting than Georgia history. I hated that stupid class."

Daniel's demeanor darkened. "One day the cat came in and laid down at the end of the General's bed. We called him Reaper, the death cat."

Daniel stumbled over his words. "Reaper knew when the next person in the nursing home would die. It was as if he wanted to say good-bye. A nurse's aide told me Reaper was in General Goren's room earlier that day—the last day I saw him alive."

Daniel's eyes became teary. "I didn't want to leave because I was afraid I might not see him again. The cat had never been wrong."

He brushed his finger along the mug's edge. "The General writhed in pain. I ran to get a doctor. Triage came in. They told me he was having a heart attack. We couldn't get the defibrillator to work. Someone ran out to get another one, but it was too late. Everything happened so fast."

"I reached over and grabbed the General's hand." Daniel banged his fist on the table. The cup rattled. Propping up his chin with his other hand, he was too choked up to continue. He buried his face in his hands.

I leaned in and touched his arm. "I'm sorry." I didn't know what else to say.

He wiped his forehead with his hand and shook his head. His voice was bitter. "I blamed myself. I know it wasn't my fault, but he was as a father to me. We knew he was going to die. I should have made sure the defibrillator worked."

I couldn't think of anything more to say to comfort him.

Daniel continued his monologue. "After that, I became depressed. They put me in a psych ward. I didn't want to speak to anybody. Then I discovered something."

"What's that?"

"A lot of the people in the ward weren't crazy. A couple were wacky, but most were like me. The staff doped up the patients so they didn't require much love or care."

"The workers wanted to make their job easier. The easiest way to do that was to make the patients passive. Drugged, they could live in an asylum where society could pretend they didn't exist."

Daniel pounded his fist again on the table. "I vowed not to be like that. I talked with the patients in the ward. I quit taking my medications. Of course, I didn't tell anyone."

"My family visited once a week and brought terrible news about the war and how the U.S. wouldn't help because Washington had too many problems of its own. It was easier to talk about that than to confront me. I was a disgrace to the family name. They had big plans for me."

Daniel glanced around the cave at nothing in particular. "One day I went into a trance. I looked out the window and a bright light shown though the opening, blinding me. When the light faded, I was some-where else, far away, though still in a hospital ward—of sorts. Where was I? I had no idea."

I stared at Daniel. "You don't belong here?"

He shook his head. "I know I'm here for a purpose. I mean, why would I be here? Do you know what the date is?"

"No," I whispered.

"Looking back from 2015, it would be two thousand years ago, and I find you here. I have no idea what's going on."

I shook my head. "I don't either. How did you end up at my father's estate?"

"After I went back in time, I discovered I could talk to patients. I could read their minds. I had never been able to do this. A prominent doctor noticed me, a kind man. Doctor Luke."

"Doctor Luke?"

"Yes. You say that like you know him."

"I saw him yesterday in a small town on the way here."

"He travels wherever he's needed." Daniel chuckled. "Strange you would see him. Anyway, Doctor Luke has a keen mind. He noticed I could communicate with the patients in an unusual way."

"Like I can talk to animals?"

"Yes." Daniel nodded. "Doctor Luke had a good friend, Theophilus, who is a prominent man with the Roman government. Theophilus asked Doctor Luke if he knew of anyone who could help a servant whose son was mute. The son's illness had taken a turn for the worse, sending the boy into fits. The doctor encouraged me to meet Theophilus. When I met Theophilus, he asked me if I'd consider going to Brutus Snyder's home and meeting his son—your half-brother, Nathan."

I nodded.

"I liked Nathan. Mr. Snyder, your father, asked me to stay. He told me if I'd also take care of the animals, he would pay me a nice wage plus room and board. That was about six months ago. So here I am. Why am I here and when or how will I ever get back—at least to my own time, is the question?"

I laughed. "That makes two of us. Maybe we were supposed to meet each other."

Daniel glanced behind me. I turned around and caught a glimpse of a body that disappeared through the doorway.

"That was Judd," Daniel said. "How much do you think he heard?"

"I told you, you should have shut the door. The jerk hates me."

"Shale, he's not the same Judd from your own time. He's Judd but a counterpart—he didn't travel here to this world as we've done."

"What?"

"I don't get it either. Perhaps multiple realities exist based on choices we've made about issues that are important to us. If we make one decision, we go down one road. If we make another decision, we go down another. Whatever choice we make has a significant impact on the reality we're dealt."

"But he knows me, and I know him. He has to be the same person."

"He's the same person—but it's like you're in a parallel universe. Suppose you had been born in this time and in this country? This would be your world."

"I still don't understand."

"I'm not saying I completely understand either," Daniel said, "but some things seem to stay the same."

"Like what?"

"Who we are, our souls, our relationships. Perhaps it's to learn what we're made of, to come to terms with issues we can't resolve any other way."

"That's very philosophical. So my father is my issue?"

"Perhaps."

"What's yours?"

"I don't know. My family isn't here except for one sister in Dothan who runs a small business. I might be related in some way to Mari, but she won't tell me how. She's afraid, as if there's a dark secret she doesn't want me to know."

"The animals—they keep talking about the king, and that the king brought me here."

"I don't know anything about a king," Daniel said, "except—"

"Except what?"

Daniel hesitated. "I don't know if it's a coincidence, but many years ago Herod killed all the babies of this area because of a sign in the stars that a great king was born in Bethlehem. Herod didn't want his authority usurped by another, but I never heard anything more about it. It does clue me in on the year."

"How is that?"

"When you put it into the historical context, it's a little eerie."

I wasn't sure I understood, but I was more interested in learning about Daniel. "Did you say you come from 2015? Did I hear you right?"

"Yes."

"You are from my future."

"And you come from 2012." Daniel raised his eyebrow. "I'm not sure I understand all of this myself." His face turned somber. "I wouldn't want to be you and relive the last three years."

"What do you mean?"

"Do you really want to know? There's war ahead. Your country's lack of leadership and socialistic leanings is to blame. Iran obtains a nuclear bomb. When Israel is attacked, the United States does nothing to help. The President lies and turns his back on the Jewish people. Islam takes over large portions of the world—bent on killing anyone who is an infidel."

"Who's an infidel?"

"Anyone who isn't Muslim. I have a friend in America who escaped Iran many years ago and married an American woman, though most of his family couldn't get out of the country. They were killed—all because they were Baha'i and not Muslim. Anyone who thinks Islam is a peaceful religion is insane."

"What is Baha'i?"

"It's a religion that embraces the prophets from all the major religions—a religion of unity. Muslims killed his family because they couldn't even accept a religion of unity in their own country."

I wasn't sure I wanted to know, but I couldn't resist. "What else happens over the next three years?"

"War, famine, pestilence, financial collapse. America suffers the most—their military decimated by spending cuts. The dollar collapses because of the mounting debt and Washington's unwillingness or inability to cut frivolous spending. China takes over as the dominant world power, and Islam seizes control of many governments. The world is aflame. When you reject God, bad things happen, sooner or later. There is always judgment."

"You scare me, Daniel. I don't know if I ever want to go back."

"It's not as if we're in paradise here." Daniel was quiet for a moment. "In some ways, you've complicated things." He gazed toward the door. "Where in the U.S. are you from?"

"Atlanta, Georgia."

Daniel smiled. "One of my distant cousins lives there. I doubt that you would know her, though."

"Who is it?"

"Rachel Franco."

"Rachel Franco?"

"Yes." Daniel's eyes lit up. "You know her?"

"She's my best friend."

Daniel chuckled under his breath. "Wow."

I sat mesmerized, thinking about all the strange coincidences. Was life a series of coincidences or was our destiny controlled by another?

"I haven't ever met Rachel but I'd love to someday. From the pictures I've seen, she's beautiful."

I shook my head. "I don't understand what's happened."

Galloping horses thundered outside the cave.

Daniel's eyes grew wide. "Your father has arrived. A moment of truth for you."

"How do you know?"

"I can read minds. Like this morning by the well. How do you think I knew something was wrong?"

"I don't know." I hoped he couldn't read mine or he would know I was attracted to him.

Daniel directed me towards the door. "Come. It's time for you to meet your father—maybe one of the reasons why you're here."

I nodded.

Outside the brightness seemed blinding after sitting so long in the dark cave. Daniel walked over to the horse tethered to a post. My father had already gone inside.

"Wait a second, and I'll introduce you—if it would make you less nervous. I'll be right back." Daniel led my father's horse to the stall and I waited impatiently. The longer I waited for Daniel to return, the more nervous I became. I glanced down at my shaking hands. Suppose this was a mistake? What would my father think of me? I didn't want to wait. I opened the back door and peered inside.

CHAPTER 15

M OMENT OF TRUTH IN A WORLD OF SHADOWS

A large shouldered man with a full beard approached. A friendly grin spread over his florid cheeks. "Shale, is that you?" His brown eyes wrinkled at the corners. "Shale!"

My heart leaped. The sound of my name on his lips. Had Brutus, my father, ever said that when I wasn't around? I tucked a strand of hair behind my ear.

He hesitated, then opened his arms and took three quick steps towards me in a warm embrace. Could that be sweet love?

"You don't know how long I've waited to do that." He stepped back leaving his hands on my shoulders and studying my face. He chuckled. "It's good to see you don't have the Snyder nose."

"The what?"

"Oh, never mind. A joke." He laughed. "At last I can see you and touch you."

"Uh." I looked at his large nose. "It's good to be here with you, too." My fingers toyed with the egg in my pocket. He didn't appear to be as my mother described him. Could I trust my feelings? As if in a mirror, I stared into his brown eyes that reflected back a part of who I was.

A door slammed behind me. I turned.

Scylla's eyes flashed. "Oh, excuse me."

Not catching her expression, my father beckoned to her. "Come here and meet Shale."

Scylla laughed. "We met yesterday."

I had hoped to have this moment with my father all to myself. I didn't want to share it with her.

My father remembered. "Oh, that's right, yes."

She glided smoothly through the room towards a bench close enough to hear us. She tossed me a fake smile and ran her hand along his broad biceps.

My father picked up a silver cup from the table and poured some wine. "Love, would you like a sip of wine?"

"Of course," Scylla said. "We must honor our visitor with a toast."

My father handed her a cup and popped a surprise kiss on her cheek.

"Love you, honey," she said.

He then walked over and sat on the bench by Nathan. Leaning back, my father stretched out his legs. "Tell me about your trip, Shale. Everything went well? No problems?"

"Everything went fine," I said glibly.

"That's good to hear." An awkward silence followed. He took several sips and burped. "It was a long trip from Jerusalem. I came as quickly as I could, once I received word of your coming."

I fumbled with the egg in my pocket, not saying anything. A few minutes passed. My father gulped down the last of his drink and set the cup on the table. "Shale, let's take a walk outside and get some fresh air."

"Sure, that sounds great." As we headed to the door, Scylla's beady eyes followed me like a radar gun.

Outside, Daniel rounded the corner. "Good afternoon, Mr. Snyder."

"Did you meet my daughter, Shale?"

Daniel smiled and nodded. "Yes, sir. A very nice young lady."

"Good, good." My father reached over and gave me another warm hug.

We left the back courtyard and headed out on the dirt road that led to the front of my father's rich estate. Without jealous ears eavesdropping, I could study him—his mannerisms, the way he walked, the inflection in his voice.

"Shale, it's good to see you. I don't want to lose you again."

How different my life would have been if he hadn't left when I was young. The gentle knocking of rocks by our sandals in the gravel was the only sound.

"Scylla and I have been married for a few years. Time passes quickly. She's the best wife I've had. Maybe after the fourth, I can get it right, huh?"

"I suppose." I wouldn't say what I really thought—like what do you see in the woman besides her fading beauty?

After a while, we turned to head back.

My father said, "I have to return to Jerusalem tomorrow. There has been a lot of trouble with the Jews. They are a noisy bunch, prone to causing disturbances. It's my job to keep the peace."

"What is it you do?"

"I'm a diplomat for the Roman government. I speak several languages—Latin, Greek and Hebrew, among others."

"You speak Hebrew?" I asked.

"Yes. It helped me to get this job."

"What about me? Am I to stay or go back?"

"You and your mother didn't discuss that?"

"No."

"Oh." My father rubbed his eyes.

Four doves flew off out of the tree nestled in the bend of the road. Worldly Crow had spooked them, eavesdropping.

My father shuffled his feet. "We'll discuss it more when I return. I shouldn't be gone long."

"How long?" I asked.

"A few days, perhaps. I left in the middle of a potential uprising, but I had to see you. I couldn't wait. Is there anything you need? Money?"

"A few days? Promise?"

"It won't be fourteen years again." He laughed. "I need to be sure we don't have a revolt on our hands. Jerusalem is restless with rumors concerning the prophecy of a new king. Thirty years ago, strange signs appeared in the heavens, and a political massacre of young babies in Galilee occurred. The prophecies have yet to be fulfilled. Some believe the time is right. A man named John the Baptist has stirred up the masses."

I wanted the answer to one question. "Why did you leave my mother?"

"Why did I leave your mother?"

"Yes."

"Let me see."

A minute passed, and he didn't say anything. I counted the goats in the field and the butterflies on a nearby bush. Would he respond?

"The truth is, I couldn't get along with your mother."

I laughed. "I can understand that. I can't get along with her either." At the expense of not making her look bad, I added, "but she means well."

"I'm sure she does," my father said blandly.

"But even if you couldn't get along with my mother," I pointed out, "you didn't have to be a stranger all those years."

"I know. That was my mistake. I should have tried."

"Why didn't you?" I persisted.

"I didn't want to interfere. She had her life, boyfriends, and then she remarried—it would have been difficult and complicated. I didn't want the conflict."

"I know she doesn't like you, but it's sad that I couldn't have a relationship with you."

My father reached over and gave me another hug. "Listen, if you need anything, Scylla will be here. Daniel takes good care of Nathan in my absence."

"Can Nathan talk—at all?"

"The only one he can talk to is Daniel."

We walked for a while without saying anything else. I was glad to be with him, but it would never be enough to make up for the fourteen years of his absence.

"Do you know what it feels like to be abandoned?" I asked.

"I didn't abandon you. I sent your mother money and sent you presents."

"They all arrived broken. Whether you call it abandonment or not, that's what it felt like. I didn't have a father like most of my friends— to do things with me, to love me, to hug me, to be there for me."

"You do now—since your mother has remarried."

"If you didn't abandon me, what did you do?"

My father shrugged. "I met your mother on a blind date. She was controlling—too controlling. We weren't made for each other."

Why was this so difficult? I needed to know the truth. I'd try again. "I used to wonder what it would be like if we met. I dreamed of spending time with you. I didn't like growing up without a father. Something was missing. I felt as if I were a doughnut with a big hole in the middle. Mother never understood me—and she sure didn't like you by the time I was old enough to realize everyone else had a father but me."

"I was always afraid—it's difficult to be rejected once, but what if it happens twice? I don't know which is worse, rejection or abandonment, but in the end, they feel the same."

My father grimaced at my bluntness. "Shale, I'm glad to see you. I really am. I won't leave you again." He hugged me reassuringly. "I hate that I can't stay here longer, but I have to head back to Jerusalem tomorrow."

I reached into my pocket fumbling for the egg. "By the way, I have something to show you."

"What's that?"

I pulled out the gift he had sent me.

A frown crossed his face when he saw the broken pieces. "How did that happen?"

"I don't know. The package arrived broken."

A dark shadow fell on us as the sun slipped behind some clouds. "Are you sure your stepfather and mother didn't break the egg?"

"What?" Why would he accuse them of such a mean thing? "I received it when the box arrived. I opened it."

He eyed me skeptically.

"Actually, everything you've sent me arrived broken."

"I'm sure they broke them."

"They didn't."

My father looked away irritated before he regained his composure. "Shale, I really am glad you're here. I never want to lose you again."

He stopped and gazed into my eyes. That instant, I believed him.

"Shale, do you need anything?"

"Yes. I'd like something to write on."

"Write?"

"Yes, so I can keep a diary."

"I can get you a reed-pen and papyrus paper."

"That would be great." My father gave me one last squeeze.

When we returned to the house, a messenger from Jerusalem had arrived on an important business matter. My father took him into his private quarters, and I waited in the veranda. They spoke another language, but I heard my name a couple of times.

I wandered about the room, picking up pieces of pottery, examining them, and setting them down, passing the time until he was finished. Why was I here? I related better to the animals than I did my own family. I felt as if I were a stranger rather than my father's daughter.

Nathan stared out the small window—which was how he spent most of the day. With our father here, he had perked up, perhaps anticipating spending time with him.

I walked over and sat beside him. Both of us were trapped in similar ways.

Scylla walked in, surprised to see me. "I thought you were still out for a walk."

"We just came back. He's talking to someone."

"Oh." She walked past us and stuck her head in the door. I wasn't sure if she understood the conversation.

She shrugged. "Mari, can you fix us another drink."

I didn't know how they could drink that horrible stuff.

"Did you and your father have a good conversation?"

I nodded.

"He's a brilliant man. I'm sure you must have inherited some of his talent. You look like him."

"That's what my mother told me."

"How is your mother?"

"She's fine." I didn't want to talk about my mother. She was nicer to me when my father was nearby. Would she talk this way to me in private?

Soon my father came out of the room with the messenger. He looked distracted—indecisive.

I didn't want to admit I was like my mother or my father. I wasn't even sure if I met one of them on the street, I'd want to be friends with either.

Regurgitating noises came from Nathan. He threw up on the floor. The suddenness caught us all by surprise. My father grabbed some rags from the table and rushed over to him.

Father patted him on the back and Nathan grunted, looking embarrassed. "It's okay, Nathan. We'll clean it up."

Scylla rolled her eyes at the mess and walked out. "I'm going to be sick," she mumbled.

I laid the rags on top of the mess.

"I'll come back later," the messenger said. Mari and I were left to finish clean-up. My father escorted Nathan off, gently speaking to him. I was encouraged that my father had compassion for Nathan. It gave me hope.

Mari smiled at me. "You're a good daughter," she said. "You have a kind heart."

Later that evening in my bedroom, I stared out the tiny window at the stars, counting how many I could see. A shooting star skimmed across the sky, and I made a wish, skeptical that it would come true. When I returned my gaze to the inside, dark cartoon characters were once again climbing the walls.

CHAPTER 16

D ISTURBING DISCOVERY

A dream awakened me. I had dreamt it before, but this time it seemed more real. Much-Afraid stood waiting for me for a very important event. She was washed, combed, and groomed to perfection. How long had it been since I held her in my arms? Were we to attend an important event together in the future?

I had been preoccupied with meeting my father. I knew Daniel was taking good care of the animals, but I had to see Cherios right away. Impatience has its virtues.

I snuck out and shivered in the cool morning air, When I opened the cave door, Cherios, Much-Afraid, and Lowly greeted me with hugs and kisses.

"It's good to see you." I wrapped my arms around Much-Afraid and plucked Cherios off the floor, setting her in my lap. I smiled at Lowly. I still didn't want to hug a pig. Then I noticed Baruch wasn't in his stall.

I glanced at the three of them. "Where is my favorite donkey?" Was Baruch outside getting some fresh air or taking a walk in the field?

"Oh, he left while the moon was still shining," Lowly said.

"What did you say?" A red panic button started blinking. Where would Baruch have gone so early in the morning?

Much-Afraid spoke up. "I can tell you what happened. I was suspicious. Maybe it's nothing."

I stood and set Cherios on the floor. "What are you talking about?"

"No, I'll tell," Cherios said. "He told me more than ya'll. He tells me everything."

"Could one of you tell me where Baruch is?"

Some of the other animals stirred as our voices alarmed them. Assassin was in the pen in the back. Did he have something to do with this?

Cherios wiggled her nose and looked brightly into my eyes. "Why are you so upset? He went to get some apples."

"Get some apples? There aren't any apples around here."

"No?"

"Start from the beginning and tell me."

Cherios took a deep breath. "Assassin told Baruch there were apples in the valley, but you had to pick them early or scavengers would get the best ones. He tiptoed out the wooden gate before anyone except me awoke. Even before ole Worldly Crow was up and before the rooster cock-a-doodle-doo'd."

"Keep going." I wished Cherios could talk faster.

"I-I knew later," Lowly said. "I just wasn't awake y-yet."

"Keep going," I pleaded.

"Assassin found an old crinkled map of the famous Apple Orchard in the valley between the Temptation Mountains near the Wilderness Pass. He promised Baruch even though it was a long journey, it would be worth it when he tasted the red apples. As Baruch left, Assassin assured him he would tell the others he was bringing them a surprise."

I glanced back at Assassin. He was asleep or pretended to be asleep —probably to avoid my probing questions.

Cherios continued. "Assassin said he would get Judd to bring in some fresh oats, and Baruch could have the big stall with the best view, although he already was in that stall. I don't know why Baruch even listened to him."

I rolled my eyes. Donkeys weren't the brightest creatures in the world, and Baruch was far too trusting to be good at even being dumb.

Cherios hopped around in a circle wringing her paws. "Baruch said he misjudged Assassin. Assassin wanted to be his friend. He promised to bring some of the apples back to Assassin—those he didn't eat."

"Did Baruch say how far it was?"

"About a half day over and a half day back." Cherios twitched her nose. "You know how much Baruch loves apples. Since he's missing the king's garden so much, he said he would do anything to eat one."

I shook my head in disbelief. "Not good. Where did he say he was going?

"The valley beyond the Wilderness Pass of the Temptation Mountains."

I leaned on the gate, staring at the empty stall beside my three faithful friends. I glanced at Assassin. He had put Baruch up to this hoax, the jealous, conniving donkey that he was.

"But even worse than that," added Lowly, "he dropped the map on the way out the door. I saw it fall out of his knapsack." Lowly held the scrunched-up map in his mouth.

"Here, let me see that." I took it out of Lowly's mouth and studied the crumpled page as I walked over to Assassin's stall.

The red donkey smiled, displaying his white pearly teeth, as if to intimidate me.

"Why is your name Assassin?"

His nostrils flared crookedly as he swished his tail. "I'm a wild jack ass, and all the jennies belong to me. There's no room for another jack ass in my territory. I will assassinate him."

Could I find Baruch in the wilderness before it was too late?

CHAPTER 17

WILDERNESS JOURNEY

The sun arched over the horizon and bathed the hills in a soft, crimson orange. The roosters were late crowing, and the silence welcomed me. Draped as curtains in the distance stood the Temptation Mountains— bold, majestic, and inviting. Assassin said it would take two hours to get there, not a half day. I planned to be back by mid-afternoon. How much of a head start did Baruch have?

I tucked the half-torn map back into my dress pocket. The well-marked road meandered easily through the hills but split into three unpaved stretches of gravel that disappeared in the mountains. I glanced around to get my bearings. The hills all looked the same. Which route would Baruch have taken?

If I went straight and took the middle road, I'd arrive sooner, though it would be a harder trek up the mountain. I made good progress for a while, but soon the climb became overwhelming. The rocky ground, barren except for a few clusters of brown weeds, was all I could see for miles, even up the mountainside. I stopped to rest on a rock beside a cactus plant. I was thirsty but wanted to save the little water I brought for later.

I longed to swim in the cool water of the king's garden as I sweltered in the heat. The sun was high and the shadows short. Without warning, pollen splattered my face and burned my eyes.

I slid off the rock, smearing the sticky goo on my cheeks. Without a wet cloth, my feeble attempts to wipe it off made it worse. Did the pollen come from the cactus plant? I took some of the little remaining water, cupped my hands, and wiped the pollen out of my eyes as best I could.

My throat burned from dryness as I kicked up the dry sand when I walked. How many people died out here? What did I know about trekking around in a desert wilderness? The farther I went, the more I wanted to turn back. Shade was sparse when it showed up—under a few scraggly trees and large boulders.

The hard surface cracked beneath me and reminded me how stupid I was for being here. Deep empty rivulets in the gullies betrayed times of flash flooding. The occasional wind that whipped up from the south offered flashes of relief, although when the wind stopped, the air became as hot as fire. Still, I pushed ahead. I wasn't going to leave Baruch here to die.

A short distance ahead, three vultures circled. I expected the stench of something dead and looked for an unfortunate victim, but all I saw was smoke bubbling from the hot surface. As I stared, rising vapors wiggled up from the ground in squiggly shapes.

The snaking vapors attracted the vultures that circled in the sky. I rubbed my eyes. Maybe the pollen from the cactus was causing me to hallucinate. When I quit rubbing my eyes, the vultures still circled, but the wavy, snake-like creatures were gone. The unexplained vision spooked me.

I pulled out the map. Less than a mile to go. I was making progress. I noted the different peaks around me—the one to the left had a little crook in its side. In the middle was a pointed one, like a church spire, and to the right was a round pancake top rock formation. South, the lower rambling hills picked back up again. I gathered five medium-size stones and plopped them down in the shape of an arrow, pointing back in the direction from which I'd come.

As I walked along the rocky path, the silence seemed eerily quiet. Shouldn't there be buzzing insects or birdcalls or the scampering of lizards? I inhaled deeply but couldn't smell anything familiar.

I pushed ahead to the top of the plateau where an unobstructed view provided a panorama from the pinnacle. A stark wilderness spread out for miles even though the map showed an apple orchard with wild honey. This confirmed my fears. Assassin had sent Baruch to his death.

I scrutinized the wasteland and caught something moving in the valley. I strained my eyes to see. Was it Baruch?

"Baruch, it's me, Shale." He was too far away to hear. I called to him three more times before he heard me.

"Eeeee ooorrrr!"

Did he know that Assassin had duped him? I ran down the rocky path to greet him.

The donkey's tired eyes popped with joy. "Miss Shale, how did you find me here?"

I pulled out the torn map. "You left this behind."

Baruch leaned over the map and scrutinized it. "I didn't know I didn't have it until I went to pull it out of my knapsack. I thought I could find the orchard anyway. Am I in the wrong place?"

"You've been duped, Baruch. There's no apple orchard here. It was a joke."

"A joke?"

The sun's heat had drained me physically and emotionally. Perspiration dripped on the map.

"I need to get in the shade before I faint." We edged over to some nearby boulders, and I collapsed in a patch of shade. Baruch, subdued, trailed behind me. I pulled out the map again and showed him where we were. Assassin had put a large "X" over the non-existent apple orchard.

"There are no apples here. Assassin lied to you. He wanted to get rid of you so you wouldn't get all of the beautiful jennies."

"What jennies?" Baruch brayed loudly, stomping the hard ground with his hind legs. He then flipped the map out of my hands with his nose and smashed it into the gravel.

"I was afraid if I didn't come after you, I'd never see you again. You and your apples. We've got to get your knapsack fixed, too, where it's torn."

Baruch snorted. "He wanted to be my friend."

"Assassin is a cruel donkey. His owner is—never mind what he is."

We sat resting for a few minutes as reality set in. Thinking about the long walk back exhausted me before we even started. "We need to go."

Baruch's ears drooped beside his crestfallen face. "I miss the garden."

As my eyes wandered across the valley, rushing waters split the silence. My heart pounded. A similar sound chased us before—when we left the garden. I scanned the horizon. Flash flooding in the desert was dangerous. The water would cascade down the mountains, overflow the wadis, and drown anything in its path.

Baruch nodded towards the mountain. "Look."

Gushing waters heaved down the slopes followed by a bolt of lightning. The flashing streak tore the desert into two dimensions, one sense of reality draped over the other. The gigantic boom echoed, shaking my sense of safety, reverberating off the mountains and fading into the valley.

The new dimension opened up as the first one pulled back, like curtains at a play, revealing something hidden within the desert. What was real? Were there two dimensions existing side by side? The fabric of my world seemed torn, like the cloth of Baruch's knapsack.

CHAPTER 18

T HREE TEMPTATIONS

The tear stretched up to the top of the mountain where two opposing forces faced each other. Blackness clothed one creature, layering him in obscurity. The other was a man with a white shawl draped over his head and shoulders. His lacerated feet were swollen from walking in the hot, dry desert. Weary, on the verge of collapse, he leaned against a rock, breathing heavily.

How could I see such detail so far away? Was I watching a movie that a mysterious director wanted me to see?

"*Hee-haw, hee-haw.* That is the king!" Baruch exclaimed. The donkey held his head high and bowed low to the ground.

"Which one?"

"The one in white. The one in blackness—oh, I bet that is an underling." Baruch dithered and dathered about, trembling one moment and singing the next.

"That is just a man," I said. "The one in white doesn't look like a king. You must be mistaken."

"No, it's him. The king. I'd recognize him anywhere."

"How can you recognize him?"

"He called my name. Once the king says your name and you listen, you never forget who he is."

I remembered the story about Baruch from *The Donkey and The King*:

"Baruch walked towards the flaming sword.

He heard the king call his name. 'Baruch.'

'I'm not afraid,' he said. 'I know the king loves me.'

Tears of Joy fell from his face and covered the flames."

"Why would he even be here?"

"I don't know," Baruch said. "Let's watch and see what happens. The king has rewarded us with a front row seat to what might be a spectacular event."

Except I wasn't sure I wanted to watch. Maybe we weren't even supposed to see it.

The dark creature's outer covering was pitch black—so gloomy that nothing could penetrate its facade.

Despite my worry, my vision, hearing, and sense of smell seemed magnified a hundred times—like an eagle soaring and spotting his next meal or a rescue dog discovering a missing child. A crow's call from beyond the mountain echoed over the valley. An ant scurried several feet away. I could see it clearly, as if my eyes were like a Nikon lens. Sweet spices from a distant town made me hungry. I assumed that's where the scent came from as I'd brought no food, and no one was cooking nearby.

Lightning pierced the sky—revealing a wild remote niche hidden in the wilderness, nearby but far away.

The vile-looking creature towered over the man. His black robe furled across the sky darkening the desert of light, hope, understanding, and knowledge.

The underling said, "If you are the Son of God, command that these stones become bread."

Stones appeared before the man in the white shawl, some in piles, and others scattered across the barrens.

"Son of God?" I repeated. "What does that mean?"

"I'm telling you, that's the king," Baruch said. "The other creature is an underling. Maybe THE underling. The underlings looted the garden and stole from the king. The king protected us and kept us safe."

The blackness contracted and expanded across the hinterlands.

The man said, "It is written. 'Man shall not live on bread alone, but on every word that proceeds out of the mouth of God.'"

"Baruch, if that is a king, a king of what country?"

"He's the king of the garden."

A longing arose within me and burned a pathway to my soul. Another reality emerged—of love, oneness, beauty, and knowledge, but a power struggle brewed. Could evil challenge goodness and win? My heart thirsted for the truth, to understand. The meaning eluded me.

In the desert, a beautiful city sprawled out across the way of the wilderness. In the center of the metropolis stood a magnificent temple. Its ornateness spoke of charm, glory, and future perfection, but where were the people? The city was empty.

The veiled creature led the man to the highest point of the building. He said, "If you are the Son of God, throw yourself down; for it is written, 'He will command his angels concerning you'; and 'on their hands they will bear you up, so that you will not strike your foot against a stone.'"

Was this man the Son of God? Where were the angels? What magic did the black creature possess? If he was so powerful, why did he want this ordinary man to call on the angels to save him?

The man replied, "It is written, 'You shall not put the Lord your God to the test.'"

The heavens shook at the man's response. The evil creature hissed and spewed profanities as if speaking the language of demons.

Angry lightening flashed across the sky. I tapped Baruch on the side. "If he's a king, is he also the Son of God? How can a king be the Son of God? He even sounded like he is God."

"Hush, just listen."

The underling took the exhausted man to the highest peak. A prism stretched across the heavens and the wilderness. A third reality emerged, a magic beyond anything I had ever seen, revealing dark secrets.

In a twinkling, the cloaked figure that I now perceived to be demonic made known all the kingdoms of the world. Temples of gold sprung up over the mountains, and all the deceptive power of the black creature's kingdom filled the air—an illusion of wealth that would fool those who did not know the difference between real and counterfeit.

How could something so vile create such beauty? The man, a willing captive, watched attentively.

The underling mocked the man's appearance and cast insults. His desperation mounted to the point of total self-absorption. "All these things I will give you, if you fall down and worship me."

"Baruch, what's happening?"

"Wait, Miss Shale. We need to see the rest."

Was he the king of the garden, as Baruch said? If he was, why was he here? Why were we the only ones to witness this? Did the powerful words stir me, or was it something else? I identified with the pauper. I knew what it felt like to be bullied, but his humility was superhuman.

The man responded, "Go, Satan! For it is written, 'You shall worship the Lord your God and serve him only.'"

A brief silence followed. "No!" the wicked creature bellowed.

Dark bat-like bodies fell from the sky, shape-shifting apparitions, without substance, and the desert floor broke apart to inhale them. A treacherous chasm opened swallowing the underlings. Screams screeched out of the hole in the ground, pathetic, whimpering gasps, and the hole collapsed in on itself, like a sinkhole. The tempter departed.

Descending from the heavens were beautiful creatures, too numerous to count, decked out in white. They wore glowing robes of dazzling splendor. As they tended to the man Baruch called a king, I watched, too awed to speak, and too stunned to know what to think.

A few minutes later, I regained my senses.

"Now you know what an underling is," Baruch said.

"A coward, a bully, a demon." I shook my head, still stunned. "Baruch, you did see all of that, right? I wasn't imagining it."

"Heehaw. Now you know the king."

"I want to meet him, Baruch. How can I?"

"Just call on him, and he'll answer you."

"Ca-ca. Shale Snyder?"

I spun around. I'd heard that voice before. On a barren rock sat a dazzling black crow. The pink backdrop of the desert silhouetted him making him look like a creature from Mars.

The crow cocked his head and flapped his wings. "Did you know that crows are among the smartest creatures in the world?"

CHAPTER 19

THE CONFLICTING WORLDS OF SHALE AND DANIEL

The bird had the most annoying habit of showing up when I was exhausted. "Worldly Crow, what are you doing here?" Did I have a tracking device around my ankle?

Worldly Crow strutted on a flat, dull rock a few feet away. "Checking on you, to make sure you're still alive. It seems some folks are ready to plan your burial. How do you think I found you?"

"Because you're smart?"

The crow looked too smug for his own good—my flattery brought out the worst in him. I stared up into the sky. The only sign anything spectacular had occurred was the dissipating hole in the clouds. I felt numb, and I didn't want to leave so soon, but life in the desert was tenuous at best. I knew it was late by the sinking sun, and we were getting close to that boundary of no return.

"What time is it?" I asked.

"*Ca-ca.* Late enough I came to find you."

Fogginess crept into my mind. Would anything like that ever happen again? Within me, hope breathed and longing remained— which compensated for all that seemed but a fabulous memory.

"What are you staring at in the sky?"

"Nothing, Worldly Crow. Nothing at all." I turned and patted Baruch on the back. "We better head back if we want to get home before dark."

As we walked down the steep mountain, a small stream percolated from a crevasse. I dipped my face in the cool water. After swallowing several gulps, I looked up over the desert and imagined the scene again —a dark creature taunting a poor wanderer whom Baruch called a king. As for the beautiful creatures that came to help the man after- wards, who else could they have been but angels?

We arrived home at dusk. My father had left for Jerusalem, putting word out to everyone to keep an eye out for me. I supposed it was good he wasn't too worried or I would have been in a lot more trouble.

I found papyrus paper and a reed-pen on the vanity in my room. I smiled. I clasped the egg in my pocket—would I ever see him again?

I sat at the table to try out my new writing instrument. I'd pretend I was Anne Frank and keep a diary—in a way I was like her, held some- where, although I didn't know where. She called her diary "Kitty." I'd name mine "Dog"—God spelled backwards.

"Dear Dog, I don't know the day, but you do. Thank you for intro- ducing me to my father—though it seems odd to meet my father at the ripe old age of fifteen. Thank you for my animal friends. Thank you for the gift of animal speak. You can take Judd away any time. Can you make Daniel like me? Tell me more about the king of the garden. Who is he? I saw him in the wilderness today. I'd love to meet him."

I put the reed-pen down and reflected on what I wrote. I was glad to be writing again. I'd be careful not to write anything too indicting.

Earlier in the day when we returned, Scylla was furious with me. "I rescued your donkey," I told her, "and returned him to the cave." I'd hope to appease her, but it didn't work.

She accused Daniel of not doing his job.

"No, he just got out," I insisted. I didn't want to get Daniel in trouble for my impertinence. To be safe, I chose not to ramble on in my diary about her foibles. What if she ever found my notes? I didn't need any more incriminating evidence against me.

After a bit, things returned to normal. I bided my time for a private moment with Daniel. When Scylla got busy with something besides stewing over me, I headed to the cave to find him. I spotted him in the field, staff in hand, watching over the sheep.

What a handsome young man. Too bad I couldn't let my imagination wander. Since he was three years older, I was too young to interest him. Besides, Mother wanted me to stay away from "older" men. She said I was too immature.

As I approached, his face brightened. "I hear you went on an animal rescue in the wilderness to find Baruch?"

"Yes."

He prodded his staff in the dirt. "A young girl should never go out alone. There are robbers and thieves and men with bad motives."

I ignored his rebuff. "Daniel, I need to tell you what happened and hope you can explain to me what it means."

He raised his brow with interest. "What do you want to tell me, and what makes you think I'll know the answers?"

"We saw something I can't explain—Baruch and me."

Daniel grinned. "I could read your mind, but it's more fun to listen to you."

I blushed. He might learn something I didn't want him to know. "Yes, let me tell you."

Daniel leaned against a palm tree and crossed his arms. "Go ahead."

I was elated to share my story. I brushed my hair back from my face and took a deep breath. "I went after Baruch in the wilderness, and soon after finding him, the sky opened up into two dimensions. Lightning peeled down the mountain and into the valley."

Daniel's eyes popped. "How could the sky open?"

I glanced up into the heavens, reliving the scene in my mind. How could I explain what I saw? "Have you ever seen evil?"

"Without a doubt."

"Baruch said the black creature was an underling—I call him a demon. The more I think about it, the more the vision disturbs me."

Daniel looked befuddled. "Tell me what you saw. I don't understand."

"The black creature wanted the man to worship him. The man seemed ordinary—except that he was exhausted and weak. The creature, who might have been a demon, tried three times to get the man to obey him."

Daniel stared at the ground, deep in thought, tapping the rocks with his staff.

I added, "Baruch said the man was the king of the garden. He must have been very hungry because afterwards angels brought him food."

"Angels?" Daniel eyed me skeptically. "What else did the demon want the man to do?"

I swallowed hard. "First, the underling told the man to turn the stones into bread. Then the underling told him to jump off a high peak, claiming the angels would save him. The man responded by saying, 'it is written.' Then the underling offered him all the wonders of the world if the man would worship him."

Daniel shook his head. "Sounds like something mystical. Nothing like that is in the Torah."

"The what?"

"Our Scriptures, the first five books of the Bible."

"The cloaked figure quoted words, and the man quoted other words back. I don't know where the words are written."

"This has you worked up, doesn't it?"

I nodded. "I wish you could speak to Baruch."

"You're very troubled," Daniel observed. "And for a sensitive girl like you, that makes it even more unsettling. But do you believe what you just told me—you aren't stretching the truth?"

"You don't?" I snapped. "How do you explain it, or explain how we got here, or why we're here? I thought you were smarter than me, but maybe not."

I stopped short. I had said too much. He'd hate me now, but I didn't like it when people didn't listen to me or take me seriously.

"I use logic to answer questions."

"How can you say that when we find ourselves back in time? Maybe logic doesn't always work."

"Maybe not," he responded tersely.

"I expected you to have all the answers." Disappointment overwhelmed me. It was easier for Daniel to attack what I saw than to explain what it meant. "Have you ever had anything like that to happen?"

"No, but I've seen weird things since I came here that I can't explain."

"I'm not making this up. Can you just try to believe me?"

Daniel nodded. "Yes."

"Who do you think the two creatures were?"

Daniel walked several feet away and stopped. He spoke a few words in Hebrew, clasped his hands, and lilted a few more phrases. "That explains one thing."

I approached him. "What's that?"

"Why this time? Why back in Roman times? Why now?"

"Yeah, why now?"

Daniel studied me. "How good are you in history?"

I laughed. "Not so much. It's boring."

"Not all of history. Let me give you a quick history lesson."

I anticipated a dull lecture.

Daniel began. "A significant person was born during the reign of Caesar Augustus. Controversy surrounded his birth—his origins. Many called him a king, and others called him the Jewish Messiah. I never took the rumors seriously because the Jewish leaders rejected him."

"Why did they do that?"

"Do what?"

"Reject him?"

Daniel ignored my question. "Could this be the man talked about in the New Testament—is what I started to say?"

"You mean the Bible?"

"Yes. I remember reading this story or seeing it in a movie. The devil tempted a prophet after spending forty days in the wilderness without food. Some called him a lunatic. I figured he was a false prophet. There have been hundreds of them throughout history. The Jews didn't need another one at that time in history when they were already so oppressed by the Romans."

"You didn't answer me, Daniel. Why did the Jewish leaders not believe the things he said?"

"They were wise in the law, and after evaluating his claims and his background, they found him not to be who he said he was."

"Suppose they were wrong?" I persisted.

Daniel appeared caught off guard—as if he believed what he believed because that's what he had always believed. "They weren't wrong. You are talking about the Sanhedrin, the most learned men of the day, including both the Sadducees and Pharisees, who didn't agree on anything, but both groups rejected his claims. They knew the Scriptures."

Daniel paused, as if still struggling to dismiss what I had just said. "At least your father is a Roman citizen— if that's the time period now. As for me, I'd better not stir up any trouble here."

"He didn't seem like a lunatic to me. Baruch called him the king of the garden."

"What does a donkey know about anything?"

"Do you believe in God?" I asked.

"Yes, of course, the Jewish God."

"How many gods are there?"

Daniel shrugged. "I believe in the God of Abraham, Isaac, and Jacob, the God who saved us from the Arabs after World War II when we were attacked. And, more recently, when God protected us against Iran—since help never arrived from our allies."

"Who is this guy, then? A lunatic, a prophet, a king, or God? The underling wanted the man to bow down and worship him."

Daniel wrote a Hebrew word with his staff in the sand. "If he's the same one spoken of in the New Testament, he's a misguided man who did a lot of good things. Some called him the Son of God. That's what got him into trouble with the Jews. Caesar didn't like him because some called him a king. There could only be one of those among the Romans. Jealousy reigned supreme."

I crossed my arms defiantly.

Daniel laughed. "Did he look like a king? Wouldn't he look like one? He sure wouldn't be wandering around in the wilderness."

"I suppose," I conceded.

"Shale, calling oneself God is blasphemy. Anyone who does so is subject to death. Maybe he's a schizophrenic, but he couldn't be the Son of God—or God."

"Suppose you're wrong? Suppose he's the Son of God?"

Daniel shook his head.

The look in his eyes pierced my heart.

Daniel continued. "We had a couple of patients in the psychiatric ward who were delusional. The nurses kept them doped up. Of course, they doped up everybody, even those who shouldn't have been. It's hard to know who someone is. They thought I was crazy, and I wasn't."

"You aren't crazy," I assured him. Curiosity got the best of me. "What did you just write in the sand?"

"God's name, that is too holy to say. God doesn't give his glory to others," Daniel added. "Maybe there's a reason for us being here." His voice trailed off as his eyes followed the disappearing road in the distance. Then he squinted several times.

"Are your contact lenses bothering you again?"

"No." He leaned in as if looking for something. "We're being watched."

"We are?" Prickles up and down my arms made me cringe. I didn't like surprises.

Daniel pointed towards the entrance to the cave. "Over there."

"By who?"

"Judd."

I followed his finger, but I couldn't tell if it was him. I strained to see. "How long has he been there?"

Daniel shrugged. "I don't know. He wants his job back and is looking for a way to make that happen."

I squinted to see but without success. "I hate him."

"You hate the Judd from your own life, time—dimension."

"Why do you think he's not the same?"

"I tried to explain this to you. Suppose you were born in this dimension. Imagine what the possibilities would be. You would still be you, with the same set of parents, but your future and your world would be different. Your past would be different in some ways, but the same in others. They are like parallel universes."

"Suppose there's a spiritual component you're missing, Daniel?"

"What would that be? I'm Jewish, and you aren't anything. Don't you think if there were something spiritual in all of this, I'd see it before you would?"

"Unless you're blind."

Daniel seemed irritated by my rebuff.

"Why are we here, Daniel? Something significant happened out there in the desert. I intend to find out what."

"And I like that about you, Shale Snyder."

He said my full name as if he meant it. "One more question for you, Mr. Scientist. If God wanted to reach you, do you think he could do anything in the universe to make that happen?"

Daniel exhaled. "Yes."

"So if you read something somewhere, like in a book, could he make it come alive?"

Daniel's eyes kindled with passion. "Yes."

"Could he transport you back in time?"

"God can do anything," Daniel said.

I turned back towards the house and searched for Judd. "Is he still there?"

"Yes. As long as he lets me take care of the animals, mainly yours, I don't care if he's around."

"You don't think he would hurt them, do you?"

"No. Not unless he wanted to make it appear as if I did it to get rid of me."

"You're scaring me."

Daniel said reassuringly, "He might be mean, but I don't think he's wicked."

I hoped Daniel was right. "Just one more question. Why would the underling offer the man everything if he would bow down and worship him? The black creature already had lots of power."

"There's good and evil in the world. The Pentateuch gives us examples of both." Daniel kicked the rocks under his feet. "The Jewish people have a rich history—we are God's chosen. I can't believe this pauper is any more than a good man—and still be Jewish. I could never give that up. It is who I am."

I stared at the ground. "I believe he's more than a good man, and I wish I was Jewish."

Daniel grabbed me by the shoulders, looked me in the eyes, and said. "You're a Roman, a good Roman citizen. That is to be valued here. If anything bad happens in the world, the Jews get blamed for it. It's almost like a curse."

The way he said it gave me goose bumps. "Why, if you are God's chosen?"

Daniel murmured, "I don't know."

CHAPTER 20

D ARK LIGHT OF THE MOON

Spring crept into summer and fall arrived. Before I realized, a year had passed. I grew taller and filled out a little, feeling more like a young woman than a gawky teenager.

My application to attend school was sent off, but even that wasn't without conflict. Scylla and my father didn't agree, and the one quick trip he made home from Jerusalem during that time to deal with it was disappointing. I barely saw him.

My father did win out on the choice of schools, but the delayed documents had yet to arrive. Scylla wouldn't tell me more. I wondered if she just didn't bother to follow through.

I settled into my new routine—doing my chores, avoiding Judd and my stepmother, spending quiet time with the animals, and enjoying long talks with Daniel when he wasn't taking care of Nathan. That was his main duty, but often when he was in the field watching the sheep, I'd join him.

It had now been a long time since my father had been home. Did he love me? If so, how could he stay away for so many months that now stretched into more than a year?

It was evening time, and I had just returned with water from the well. Scylla called me into her private quarters. I set down the pail and walked past Nathan, who sat alone on the bench, rocking and crying.

Scylla's voice was sharp. "Sit over there."

I grabbed the bench and plopped down on the edge. What was percolating in that dark mind of hers?

"How dare you dishonor your father's name, after all he's done for you?"

"What are you talking about?" I looked around, embarrassed for anyone to hear.

Scylla held a drink in her hand and swayed as she addressed me. Her bloodshot eyes bore into me. "You know what you did. I thought you were a lady. You're a tramp of the worst kind."

"What?"

"Judd told me about you and Daniel."

I stared at her. "What about Daniel? What are you talking about?"

"All the time you spend in the cave, sneaking in when no one is around. He said Daniel has made you crazy. He hears you talking in there, nonsense stuff, as if you could talk to the animals. We know Daniel came from the asylum, and he needs to go back there. I dismissed him this morning."

"You what?"

"I told him to pack up his stuff and leave. We don't need a lunatic like that around here."

"I thought you liked Daniel."

She ignored me. "Do you know what they do to a woman with loose morals?"

She didn't wait for me to answer. "I know you're from a distant country, but here they stone girls. Is that what you want?"

I shook my head.

"Word is out about you. I'd hate to see your splattered body sprawled out on the road. It would destroy your father's reputation, cost him his job, and my inheritance—unless Judd gets it first. If I have my way, that won't happen. I need to protect you. From now on, you'll stay where I can see you."

"Judd gets what?"

She didn't answer me.

I had no idea what she was talking about. So Judd convinced her I was a tramp even though Daniel had never once been alone with me. Even in the cave, he always insisted the door be open—probably why Judd overheard too much.

Scylla wanted to lock me up, as if I were a bird in a cage. I bet she'd get rid of me if I weren't Brutus's daughter. "Where is Daniel?"

"He's gone back to the loony house where he belongs."

"You mean to Doctor Luke?"

She eyed me suspiciously. "How do you know him?"

I ignored her question. "What about Nathan?"

Scylla waved her hand in the air. "Judd can take care of him."

"Like he took care of the animals?" Though Daniel refused to admit it, I knew Judd's care was just short of abusing them.

Scylla clumsily set down her drink and stomped her foot. "I'll not let you talk to me like that."

I fidgeted with the egg I still kept in my pocket.

"You can't even start school next week. The school rejected your application until we obtain your complete records, which your mother has refused to release. Doesn't matter. I heard you were a lousy student anyway."

"I could study here on my own," I offered.

"If you were motivated enough. Your father is attempting to get an exception—he has the clout, he just doesn't have the time to meet with the school officials."

"Are you done?" I asked.

"As done as I'll ever be."

I walked to the door. Nathan sat on the bench with tears streaming down his face. Why didn't I ask Daniel more questions about my brother? How much did Nathan know? Without a way to communicate, his thoughts would remain a mystery.

I slid over on the bench and hugged him. Did my father care about Nathan? Scylla would never send word about how upset he was. Nathan must have overheard Scylla talking with Daniel when she fired him.

Could my brother become violent if driven to exasperation? He was an annoyance to me when I first arrived, the guttural sounds he uttered because he couldn't talk. Now I squeezed his hand to comfort him.

I could feel Scylla's presence behind me, her fiery eyes spewing bullets into my back.

I whispered. "I'll see you tomorrow, Nathan."

He nodded.

After climbing the stairs, I paused—the dark memory returned and taunted me again.

Collapsing on the bed, I pulled the blanket up around my shoulders. Even though I wasn't cold, I couldn't quit shivering. Would I ever see Daniel again? Why hadn't he said good-bye?

I took out the two golden nuggets from underneath the covers and examined them. How much were they worth? Even these couldn't buy what I wanted—to see Daniel one last time and escape from my imprisonment. Where was the king in all of this?

The curse—that was it. I hated Judd. I conjured up images of knocking him down those stairs that haunted me. How could I get back at him?

I turned over the golden nuggets in my hand. Even in the dark light of the moon, their beauty transcended the shadows. Were they beautiful because they were valuable? No, it had to be more than that. They came from the king's garden, and that was what made them beautiful. I could use them for money and run away—maybe start a new life.

And leave the animals here? I wanted to see my father one more time. If I ran away, I might never see Daniel, whom I fancied I loved, again.

I returned the golden nuggets to their safekeeping in the folds of the blankets. I couldn't leave. I needed to say good-bye to Daniel. I arose, walked over to the table, and picked up the sheet of papyrus on which I'd been writing. I began today's entry:

. . .

"Dear Dog, why did you put me in this hole in the wall? What do you want from me? Why did you give me such a hateful stepmother? If it weren't for Daniel and the animals, I'd be beside myself with grief. Please show me what to do. Show me you care."

I stood and peered out the small window. Where was the king of the garden? Did he return to his own kingdom, or was he still out there? The hills spread out on the horizon as far as I could see.

No, I wouldn't leave. I wouldn't give up. I would sneak down to the cave at night and visit the animals when Judd was asleep. It wasn't like me to give up so easily. Besides, there was no way I'd leave without seeing Daniel one last time.

I composed more words from my thoughts as I walked back to the table:

"Dear Dog, you must have a sense of humor. Who else would send me back in time to meet a rabbit, a dog, a pig, and a donkey? To a land where a powerful king roams like a pauper and a handsome young man has smitten me with love. So I've met my father, but what about you? Don't leave me here."

CHAPTER 21

WORLDLY CROW – FRIEND OR FOE

Fever confined me to my quarters for the next three days. I lay in bed shivering one moment and sweating the next. The housemaid, Mari, was kind and brought me fresh water and comforting words. How could she live here and be so happy? Did she see the world through rose-colored glasses to hide something?

"Your father will be happy to see you when he returns," she said. "I must get you well." She smiled and turned my head, patting my hot cheeks with a cool cloth. "If you ever need anything, you come to Mari. I'll help you, okay?"

I nodded.

She sang a soothing song as she dried my face. Her melodic voice touched my soul as her sweet singing put me to sleep.

Later that afternoon, Worldly Crow plopped on the windowsill. "*Ca-ca.* How long are you going to feign sickness?"

"What? I'm not pretending to be sick, you fool." Indignant, I rolled over on my bed.

"What should I tell your animal friends? They are worried about you."

"Tell them I'm fine, and I'll sneak down there to see them tomorrow morning."

"Sneak?" he repeated.

"Yes. I'm not supposed to leave my room."

"Do you need anything?"

"Yes. My father."

The crow cackled several times. "You must think I'm a miracle worker."

"How about Daniel? Do you know where he is?"

"He left. The witch ran him off, ran him off for good this time."

I turned and faced him squarely. "Do you know where he went?"

"I saw him head to the village where I met you with Baruch," the crow cackled. "That was a delicious fish. Should go back and get another."

I lay still. My head hurt from the fever. Could Daniel be with Dr. Luke? I was too sick to go after him. What would I say anyway? "I'm madly in love with you and I miss you"? Or the reason he was hired in the first place—"Nathan needs you." I groaned.

"*Ca-ca.* Need anything?"

I shook my head as I lay on the blanket. "Make Judd's life as miserable as possible."

Worldly Crow flapped his wings and took off. I half-wished he'd stayed. Loneliness stalked me like a rebuffed lover. I wanted to visit the animals but was too depressed. Perhaps a good night's rest would refresh me.

CHAPTER 22

B ULLIES AND DEMONS

The next morning before dawn, I climbed out of bed and tiptoed down to the cave. As I approached the door, disgruntled voices alarmed me. I drew closer.

"Can't you two go someplace else to discuss this?" a rooster crowed. "The sun hasn't even risen yet."

I peered around to make sure no one saw me while I was eaves-dropping. Lowly pleaded, "I-I don't want to go by myself. Can't you come with m-me?"

I cracked the door.

"Go away." Cherios burrowed into the haystack in the corner of the stable. Her white ears protruded out the top.

Lowly crept over and bumped the bale with his backside. Cherios jumped out of the hay and zigzagged around the stall. "I don't want to go with you."

Lowly persisted. "Look, Cherios, we need to do something or

we're going to starve. The pigs next door might share some garbage we could eat."

"Leftover garbage? I'm not going on a long walk to eat garbage." Cherios licked her clean white fur. "You're a pig. You eat all the garbage you want over there and bring me back some fresh carrots."

"I-I don't want to go by myself."

"And you don't worry about getting lost? Have you ever been over there?"

I closed the door behind me and took a few steps into the room. The cave was not as tidy as when Daniel took care of things. "What's going on? What is this about not enough food?"

Baruch whinnied. "Miss Shale, you're going to get yourself in trouble. If Judd sees you, you'd better run for the hills."

With Daniel gone, I wasn't allowed in the cave. Judd didn't like the pig, and the rabbit annoyed him. If he had his way, he'd probably eat them for breakfast. Assassin looked as plump as ever. Having enough food wasn't the problem—it was just going to the wrong animals.

Lowly headed towards the door as if he expected me to open it.

"Wait," called Cherios.

Lowly grunted and turned around.

Cherios pounced to the door. "I'm coming with you."

"I am, too," I said.

"Both of you?" Lowly wiggled his curly tail.

Cherios nodded confidently, "We'll find something along the way."

The animals looked relieved from their burdensome spirit. I walked to the back of the stable and kissed Baruch on the nose.

"Not enough oats," he complained.

I inspected the cave, looking for animal feed. "Do you know where Judd stores it?"

"Towards the front."

After searching several containers, I found a little and poured the oats into Baruch's feeding trough. "At least you won't starve for one more day."

"Thank you, Miss Shale."

Much-Afraid joined us also. It would be the first time in a long time we had been away from my father's land. I still felt a bit warm with fever, but I wouldn't let it ruin the day.

Cherios's constant chatter was delightful. She commented about everything as she hopped from rock to rock. "And the king made all kinds of trees to grow out of the ground—trees pleasing to the eye and good for food. Now we just need to find the food."

"I hope we can," Lowly said. "My stomach is growling."

Cherios hopped onto a log and exclaimed, "Trust in the king, hope unswervingly, love extravagantly. And the best of all these magnificent things is love."

"There's not a lot of love around here," Lowly grunted. "Especially for pigs. If we aren't careful, we'll end up on somebody's plate for breakfast."

"In the garden, nobody gets eaten." Cherios groaned. "It's all because I hid in Baruch's knapsack that I'm here."

"It could be worse," I said.

"Worse? The worst thing in the world is to be separated from the king's love." Cherios caught herself from becoming bitter. "We must bring a little bit of love here and represent the king." Tears gathered in her eyes. "Do you think we'll ever see him again?"

"I saw the king when I was with Baruch once in the wilderness, but that was quite a while back." I added, "He didn't look like a king even though Baruch said it was him. He was being taunted by a bully." I walked along for a bit, lost in thought. "Did the king visit you in the garden?"

"He was the gardener," Cherios exclaimed. "He'd come down from the mountaintop and tell us fabulous stories. He's the best story-teller in the whole universe."

"What's at the top of the mountain?" I asked.

"His mansion. Many rooms fill his house. He's a magnificent carpenter. He told us he still had many rooms to build. He was preparing a place for everyone to come and stay with him. He promised someday there would be many, many more people living in the garden."

"I wish I could see him again," I said.

"Me, too. I would know him anywhere," Cherios stated emphatically. She added, "Sometimes the king would leave the garden and go to a distant land. I never knew where he went." Cherios sighed. "I miss his love most of all."

I thought about Cherios's words. "I wish I'd met the king when I was there. Maybe someday I will."

We walked for a little longer as I lamented about what could have been. To keep the mood upbeat, I added. "It's beautiful here, too, Cherios, just in a different way."

No one said anything else as we hiked along the hillside until two blood-curdling cries pierced my ears. Much-Afraid scrambled close to me.

"What was that?" I asked.

A sparsely-clothed man lumbered towards us. His long and dirty hair attracted flies that swirled about his head. His weathered hands were marred with sunspots and his fingers were knobby and thick. Bruised wrists showed tell-tell signs of abuse, as if shackled in chains. He reminded me of an animal—a beast that ate grass. The man's eyes flashed contempt—a hate beyond ordinary dislike, a hate that wanted to kill.

Shocked at the man's appearance, I stood still. Much-Afraid came between us to prevent the wild man from drawing nearer. She raised her tail and snarled.

The man stopped once he saw the dog. "Don't hurt me," he cried. His plaintive words pricked me. I pitied the man, but fear seized me when he came closer. Much-Afraid swooshed towards him.

"No, Much-Afraid, come back here." She ignored my pleas.

Cherios and Lowly ran the other way to redirect the man away from Much-Afraid. Just as Much-Afraid charged, the man turned, escaping within inches of her clutches. I screamed, fearing one of them would get hurt. Soon the man ran off, however, and Much-Afraid and the others returned.

"Are you okay?" the dog asked.

"Yes." I brushed down my dress with my hands, as if I could brush away fear.

Cherios hopped towards me. "The man seemed like an underling."

"An underling?" I repeated. "The last time I heard that word was the day Baruch and I saw the demon and the king in the wilderness." I grabbed Much-Afraid around the neck and hugged her. "Thanks for saving my life." We sat and rested on the hill to catch our breath.

In the distance, a large herd of pigs grazed. A lake bordered the east side of the hill. On the other side, the land was vacant except for an abandoned cemetery overtaken by weeds. Yellow buttercups and dandelions had sprouted up in between the blades of grass. I broke off a stem of one and blew the seeds into the air. The breeze carried them towards the lake.

Cherios hopped on a rock, wiggled her nose, and sneezed. "Do we have to go any farther?"

I studied the herd of pigs ahead. Where were the owners? I didn't see a herder. With all the wild animals around, they must be close by.

Lowly meandered over the hill to approach them. One of the large boars asked. "Who are you?"

"I'm Lowly. Your neighbor to the west."

"So, what's on your mind, Little Oinky?" The boar laughed.

I cringed. Poor Lowly. He was so insecure and intimidated by others. Even in the animal world, pigs were scorned. I wanted to help him, but I couldn't do anything with a wild boar. I waited for Lowly to answer the brute, but he was unable to put two words together—even in pig language.

"Scared piggy, uh?" Several of the pigs roared. I flinched. Bullies, they were.

"L-listen to me," Lowly began. After clearing his throat, he continued hoarsely. "I'm very hungry."

A black boar stepped forward, dwarfing Lowly by his enormous size. "What did you say?" He spat in Lowly's face. "Oh, sorry about that, my neighborly friend. I had to clear my throat."

Lowly wiped his snout on the grass. Pig bullies were like bullies at school. Their words stung. My stomach soured as I watched, but I was proud he didn't run away.

At last, a few words tumbled out. "I-I'm very hungry. I brought along my friends, Much-Afraid and Cherios." Lowly nodded towards us. "Can we sh-share your food, a few scraps? We would be obliged by your kindness."

"Share our food with you?" The boar interrupted. "You think you can just mosey up to us and steal our leaves, fungi, roots, eggs, and earthworms? This is our hill."

Lowly inched away from the bully.

The boar addressed the other pigs. "Did you hear that? He wants some of our food because he's hungry." He gawked. "Look at that silly bunny and stupid dog."

The pigs laughed.

Lowly tried again. "We won't eat much, just a little."

Before he could say another word, a heavy-weight sauntered up to Lowly and stared him down.

"So, let's settle it here and now. This is our land, you're on our turf. You want our land. That's it, isn't it?"

"No, no, not at all," Lowly pleaded.

"Get off our hill—now."

Lowly ran back to Cherios, who sat perched on a rock cleaning her paw. As conflicted as I was, I dared not go near the brutes. Being charged once by a mad man was enough. Plus, they didn't know I spoke pig talk.

Then Cherios stood on her hind legs as she looked at something far away. I followed her eyes to an overgrown cemetery. The familiar man, who had threatened us before, burst out of the shadows. He stumbled about on the hill as if he were out of his mind.

I was horrified. The man lived among the tombstones. What had he done to bring such a curse upon himself? Had he always been homeless?

The man's wailings increased. He darted from tomb to tomb, flailing his arms. What afflictions drove him to live here? His petulant eyes found me. I froze. He then turned and ran towards the pigs, scattering them on the hill.

Much-Afraid stayed beside me, ready to charge him again if he approached.

"What's wrong with him?" Much-Afraid whispered to Lowly.

"Look over there," Lowly said. "I-I see a boat on the lake."

I peered towards the shoreline. The wind was calm and the water gently ebbed back and forth. A fishing boat pulled up. Two fishermen dropped an anchor and secured their belongings. A third man stood by surveying the area.

It was about this time that the pigs' herders ran down the hill. They approached cautiously, probably more out of concern for the welfare of their livestock. They must have heard the man's cries.

The crazy man ran towards the boars.

"Get him out of here," one of the shepherds shouted, "before he kills our pigs."

"We chain him night and day," another one said, "but he breaks free."

"We should kill him and put him out of his misery." All the while, the fishermen by the lake watched.

Attempts to corral the wild man were unsuccessful. Everyone was afraid to approach him. He foamed at the mouth like a rabid animal. The possessed man then raced towards the lake. He uttered nonsensical words at the fishermen. The one he approached took great interest in him.

Cherios bobbed up and down, wringing her paws and dancing. "That is the king. The king is here among us!"

CHAPTER 23

K ING OF DELIVERANCE

"Are you sure?" I asked.

"Once you've met the king, you never forget him."

The possessed man fell prostrate before the anglers. In a loud, plaintive voice, the besieged man cried out. "What do you want with me, king of the most high? Swear that you won't torture me."

"Torture—what is he afraid of?" I asked.

His words haunted the lake like a siren's mournful calls.

A familiarity seized me. Déjà vu. The wilderness memory exploded in my mind.

The king said to him, "Come out, you evil spirit."

Were there underlings roaming the earth looking for an unfortunate victim? Captivated by the king's eyes, the anguished soul stood still for the first time in front of the fishermen.

From off the lake, a breeze stirred, slowly at first and then gaining momentum. Like onionskin, vaporous creatures peeled from the brain of the madman, and the swirling wind tore at the naked and exposed shape shifters. The black, formless creatures were like bats without bodies.

The dark beings smelled rancid, and the awful odor settled over everything. The demons cowered submissively before the king. The creatures hissed, screeched, and made themselves fools. The fearful pig herders withdrew a safe distance.

"What is your name?" the king asked.

"My name is Legion," one of the demons replied, "for we are many."

The king's power and authority over the spirits was omnipotent. The underlings knew him. They knew the king. The muscles in my shoulders tensed, and my legs twitched. Much-Afraid hid her face under my arm.

The demons begged. "Please, do not send us out of the area." They pointed to the pigs. "Send us among the pigs. Allow us to go into them."

At the king's command, they fled from the man and entered the herd. Their formless bodies slid inside the pigs. I shuddered. The pigs shook violently. The herd, numbering in the thousands, stampeded down the steep bank and headed straight into the lake.

The herdsmen watched their valuable livestock disappear, and they shouted accusations at the king. "By whose authority did you drown our herd?"

They flailed their arms at the anglers, and the shepherds traipsed back up the field resolute for answers. "Who is this man that sends pigs into the lake? By what authority does he do such things?" They continued to argue among themselves.

At first, Cherios, Lowly, Much-Afraid and I were too stunned to speak. Cherios spoke first. "Lowly, that is the king, the king of the garden. He's here. The king is here among us."

"J-just as Baruch told us," replied Lowly, "But I didn't believe him. I-I mean, I sort of did, but now that I've seen with my own eyes, I believe better."

We continued to watch, but the deranged man's appearance was now strikingly different. He had washed his hair, face, and hands in the lake and sat quietly at the king's feet. One of the others brought him clothes.

The cemetery prisoner no longer flailed about like an ox in distress. For the first time, a faint smile covered his face—a face alive with hope. Thankfulness exuded from his pores. A miraculous cleansing transformed more than the man's outward appearance—the king set him free.

By this time, crowds of people swarmed the hillside, having heard the herdsmen's rants.

"Please leave us," they cried. "We don't want you around here."

We hung around for a few hours, but I was too afraid to get close to the king. Besides, others wanted his attention—and I wasn't sure what I would say. Torn between wanting to be near him yet afraid to get too close, I lingered, watching and hoping someday I'd be brave enough to approach him.

Later in the afternoon, the fishermen began preparations to leave, but the cemetery man the king healed ran up to him and begged. "Please, let me go with you."

The king said, "Go home to your family. Tell them what I did for you and how I had mercy on you." So the man went away to do as the king instructed.

Soon the fishermen unhooked their boat and left. Sadness filled me that I didn't meet the king. Would I have another chance?

I was drawn to him in a way I didn't understand. Who was he that even the underlings obeyed him?

On the way home, Cherios was unusually quiet. Lowly kept mumbling, "I-I know you're the king, I-I believe you're the king, I accept you as the king," until Cherios asked him why he felt like he had to say it so many different ways.

"Suppose I didn't do it right the first time," Lowly replied.

"Do what the first time?" Cherios asked.

"Suppose he didn't hear me?"

"Lowly, the king heard you the first time."

"Are you sure?"

"Of course I'm sure. I know the king. Whether the king is in the garden or here or there, the king hears, knows, and is everywhere."

Despite Cherios's assurances, Lowly persisted in his fears. "The pigs wouldn't listen to me. If they had, I'd be-been feeding with them when the demons entered them." And he kept on repeating, all the way home, "I believe you're the king," but he still wasn't sure the king heard him.

"Help me with my unbelief," Lowly whispered.

Much-Afraid had taken off on a romp and now returned with a "present."

"What's in your mouth?" I asked.

"Oh, Much-Afraid, that is disgusting," Cherios chided.

I examined Much-Afraid more closely. "Are you going to eat that?"

The mouse's tail dangled over her snout. She chomped it down and gulped a couple of times. The wiggly tail disappeared in her throat.

"I don't need to worry about you starving," I chuckled.

As we headed back to the cave, I admired the green rolling hills. The sheep grazed peacefully, and the blue sky, dotted with white puffy clouds, stretched out past the horizon. Inhaling the fresh air lifted my spirits as I remembered Daniel and the good times we had together. Now that he was gone, I was on my own. My father was too busy to come home, and Scylla falsely accused me of everything. In Daniel's and my father's absence, I felt responsible for Nathan.

What did I want? If I knew, would I be willing to risk everything to obtain it? I gazed at the lake—where was the king headed? I wished I knew the lake's secrets. If he was the king from the garden, how did he get here? He seemed powerful in some ways but not in others.

I was stuck at an impasse. I couldn't get Daniel out of my mind. What would happen to Nathan? And why had I killed Judd's dog when I was just a kid? Could the king help me to get over it? If he could, how could I meet him in the future?

I had been too fearful today to show my face, too guilty about my past to approach him. Now a plan formed in a secret place in my mind. Would I be willing to risk everything?

A gentle breeze touched my face, like the hand of God, energizing the desires of my heart. Yes, I could do it. My life depended on it. I held up my fist and shook it in the air. "If you are really a king, show yourself to me."

Tears welled up in my eyes and I began to weep. Much-Afraid lumbered over and pawed at my dress. I scratched her behind the ear. "You love me, don't you?"

She barked happily. "Of course I do."

CHAPTER 24

TRUTH EXPOSED IN MULTIPLE REALITIES

Several weeks went by as I struggled with fear. Fear of approaching Judd. Fear of asking Daniel. Fear of facing the king. Fear of failure. Fear of the unknown. Fear of making a fool of myself.

I wrote in my diary today:

"Dear Dog, please help me to be successful, if this is your will. Why should Nathan be so miserable if you can heal him? How hard it must be not to be able to talk. Daniel said you could do anything. Does that mean you would heal Nathan if we brought him to you?"

I hid my diary and headed downstairs to finish my chores. Later, I waited outside the cave for Judd. I had seen him enter earlier. My heart raced, and my dress felt sweaty as I anticipated my next step. I smacked at the gnats that hung annoyingly around my face. How much longer would he be? I didn't know if he would go along with my plan, so I brought something just in case he needed convincing.

The door opened, and Judd walked out. He was surprised to see me but quickly regained his composure. He glanced at my fisted hand.

"What do you want?" he asked.

I took a deep breath. "I need your help."

He stepped down the stairs and strolled past me. "You come to me for help?"

"I need to go to Daniel."

He laughed. "You seemed to be doing quite well with him without my help."

"I need you to cover for me with Scylla."

"Cover for you? What does that mean?"

"Must I say it more plainly—I want to bribe you."

Judd laughed. "Are you trying to trick me to get him back?"

"I don't think he would come back to me even if I had magical powers."

"You don't have any money, so what could you give me as a bribe?"

I exploded. "I do have something, but first, tell me, why did you lie about Daniel and me?"

Judd advanced towards me, but I backed away. Much-Afraid ran up and growled at him.

"It's okay, Much-Afraid." I reached down and patted her reassuringly on the head.

"I didn't lie about you."

"Yes, you did. You told Scylla lies about Daniel and me, made up stories about us having a relationship. She told me what you said." My anger grew, and I couldn't stop the poison.

"I didn't need to tell her that."

"What are you talking about? Quit talking in riddles."

"You were given to me before you and your mother ran off."

"What?"

"Prearranged marriage. You know what the custom is here. I

thought you had returned to honor the contract. Didn't your mother explain that to you?"

I picked up a fist-sized rock and threw it at him. "You perverted liar! How dare you say such a thing."

"It's true. I was glad you had returned. The contract is for the end of next year, when you turn seventeen."

"Marry you?"

Judd smiled. "There's a huge dowry for you—you had to return, to keep Scylla from getting all that money."

I imagined becoming his slave and cringed. "Never!" I screamed.

Judd walked up to me and laid his hand on my shoulder.

"Get away from me, you animal." I shoved him with my elbow as I stepped backwards.

He persisted, taking a couple of strands of my long hair and wrapping them around his finger.

"Stop it."

Before I could do anything, Much-Afraid ran over and sank her canine teeth into his leg, tearing the flesh.

Judd winced, falling to the ground. "Get that dog off of me," he shouted, "before I kill it."

"You wouldn't dare," I shrieked.

Judd grabbed his leg with one hand and flailed at Much-Afraid with the other.

"Let him go, Much-Afraid," I commanded her.

Much-Afraid backed off though her curled lips still snarled. Judd scooted away, grabbing his injured leg. His torn skin displayed nasty puncture marks as the blood oozed.

"Why did you come to see me?" Judd covered the gash with his fingers to stop the bleeding. I felt woozy watching the red blood trickle. I glanced away. Memories from the hallway and bathroom returned. That seemed like ages ago.

"I want you to take care of the animals while I'm gone. I'm taking Baruch with me, and you must tell Scylla that I've gone to Jerusalem in search of my father. That way she'll take good care of Nathan if she fears a bad report when my father returns."

"Is that all?"

"That's a lot for you." I pointed my finger. "And if you do one thing to hurt Cherios, Lowly, or Much-Afraid while I'm gone, I'll kill you." I glared at him, inhaling deeply, as if I were ready to murder him with all the venom locked up inside of me.

Judd's gray eyes steamed.

How many years had it been since I was now sixteen? How much of that hate was because of me?

"He's with Doctor Luke. That's all I know," Judd said.

"That's what Worldly Crow told me."

"Worldly Crow?"

My face grew hot. A slip of the tongue. "Can you please get Baruch ready for me? I–I don't know about all of those things."

"Why shouldn't I tell your stepmother the truth? Why do you expect me to lie for you?"

"You already lied once. What difference is it to you if you lie to her again?"

Blood covered Judd's hand, and he winced in pain. "I told you, I didn't lie to her. She didn't know you were already given to me. She ran Daniel off. Or not, depending on your point of view."

"You didn't say one word about us having a relationship?"

"No. But—"

"But what?"

Judd looked away evading my question. "I think it was mutual."

"What was mutual?"

"Daniel thought it was best to leave."

"Why?" I glared at Judd, angry that he was stonewalling me.

"Shale, as I said before, you were chosen for me. When Daniel heard about it, he said he needed to go."

"Why?"

"Shale, are you blind? He likes you, for goodness sake, and he can't have you. Now please let me clean up my leg before it gets infected or I bleed to death."

I felt sorry for Judd. I was the source of much of his suffering, but I would not let go of my own pain to embrace his. "Is this all about the dowry that you want to marry me, Judd? Answer me that question. You hate me."

"No, I don't hate you. And yes, there's a contract."

"So that's it, huh? Everybody wants my father's money." I slammed my foot in the dirt and particles flew up and hit Judd in the face.

"Why did you do that? You don't throw dirt in a man's face when he's down."

"You can't have me, you hear that? Ever! Besides, I don't live here, and I plan to return home. Soon." I folded my arms in front of me and added a "humph" at the end, to make the point.

"If you want me to help you, I want money in return, which you haven't got. I'm putting myself out there lying for you. Your step-mother is evil."

"What do you know? We agree on something." I stood in front of Judd's face, but far enough away that he couldn't grab me. I held up the golden nugget. The stone dazzled in the sunlight. The attraction of the nugget was powerful. Judd stared.

"Where did you get that?"

I tossed it back and forth in my hands. "You wouldn't believe me if I told you."

"That's worth a lot of money." His eyes followed the nugget as I flipped it like a pancake. "Careful, don't drop it," he cautioned, as if he were already claiming it as his own.

I laughed. "It's not going to break."

"You wouldn't want to drop something so valuable, especially if you're going to give it to me."

I popped the golden nugget in my pocket. "You make up that story, take care of my animals, get Baruch ready, and I'll give this to you when I return with Daniel."

"Suppose he doesn't return?"

"You better hope he does if you want your golden rock."

"Why are you bringing him back here?"

"That's for you to figure out. Give Nathan some love also. He's depressed."

Judd nodded. "Do you have any more of those?"

"I'm not going to tell you. I want to leave as soon as possible."

"Can you help me get up?" Judd asked.

"No, but I'll bring you some water to put on your leg and some cloths for bandages. So I can get out of here."

"Do you know the way to Doctor Luke's?" Judd asked.

"I need a map—if you have one you can give me."

Feeling encouraged and thankful that I would soon be leaving, I ran back to my room and jotted in my diary:

"Thank you, Dog. I knew you would come through for me. Now please help me to find Daniel. Bring me success. May I call you Abba?"

CHAPTER 25

C AN SHALE WOO DANIEL

Within an hour, with a water-stained map in hand, Baruch and I set off for Dothan, passing through the terraced hills of Samaria. Despite the dangers of thieves and bandits, I'd find Daniel. Was it coincidental that I had seen Dr. Luke on the way to Nazareth?

Baruch moseyed along at a comfortable pace. "Miss Shale, I don't think Daniel will come back."

"We'll have to make him. Why are you so negative about it?"

"It doesn't work to have two men in love with the same beautiful young lady."

"What do you know about such things? Besides, I'm doing this for Nathan."

"Of course," Baruch continued, "I don't think Judd is in love with you. He wants your father's money. Daniel is another story."

I remembered the words from Shakespeare's play we had been studying in English.

"All the world's a stage.
And all the men and women merely players
They have their exits and their entrances
And one man in his time plays many parts
His acts being seven ages."

It was time to make a dramatic entrance and assume my part. I must woo Daniel back—I'd never let Judd marry me for my father's money. I didn't want to be just a player. I wanted to be a heroine.

We traveled for a while and at last came to Dothan. I glanced down at my dress and remembered the young woman, Martha, who picked it out for me. A couple of years had passed since we had last been here.

We approached the merchant's bazaar, and I searched for Martha's booth. I couldn't remember where it was. If I used that as a landmark, though, I could find the inn more easily. I peered into the storefronts reminiscing as we crossed the street. Then I saw Daniel and started to rush over to him, but who was that woman he was talking to? Martha —was that her? Daniel's mannerisms were flirtatious and too familiar.

Rage and jealousy consumed me. Hurt, anger, confusion, and disappointment overwhelmed me. What was I doing here? Was I here to help Nathan or to satisfy my own longings? The truth was painful. Martha laughed as he leaned over the counter. Then Daniel hugged her and stepped away, as if he were about to leave. I nudged Baruch before Daniel saw us—I was too embarrassed to approach him right now. My face would say it all.

Did Baruch notice? Should we turn around and go home? So Daniel had a girlfriend. Why wouldn't he? After all, he was a good-looking dude. What was so wonderful about her? I made an ugly face towards them as we headed away from the area.

Would I give up now when we had traveled this far? "Keep going," I ordered Baruch. I patted him on the back. If he saw Daniel and

Martha, he wasn't saying. Maybe I was a fool to be here, but even fools can help others, and I was here to help Nathan even if I had hoped for more.

A little later, we arrived at Jacob's Inn. The same two men lay on mats as before—for the last year and a half to two years. There were also two new patients. Where was Dr. Luke? I'd pretend I hadn't seen Daniel at all. Maybe Dr. Luke would inquire for me. I didn't want to be embarrassed.

"Wait for me here, okay, Baruch?"

"I'm not going anywhere without you, Miss Shale."

I tethered him to the post and patted him on the head. "I'll be right back."

Proper etiquette was tricky—who I could talk to, who I shouldn't talk to. Manners back home were hard to remember, but here it was worse. Everybody hated somebody. The Jews hated the Samaritans, the Romans hated the Jews, and who did the Samaritans hate? Maybe it was the Jews and the Romans. Shoot—who cared? I walked up to an elderly man lying on a cot with a deformed leg.

"Excuse me, sir, but have you seen Doctor Luke today?"

The old man eyed me awkwardly, squinting in the sunlight. "Be back soon," he said. "He went off with a young man—let's see, his name was Daniel, I believe."

"Thank you, sir."

I headed back to Baruch. "Doctor Luke's patient said he would be back soon." I fidgeted with Baruch's reins as we waited. Just act normal, I told myself. Dumb. I was good at that.

"I see Daniel now!" Baruch exclaimed.

"Where?" Then I spotted him also, conversing with Dr. Luke. Daniel and the doctor were gesturing with their hands and walking slowly. I waited impatiently.

A couple of minutes later, Daniel was within earshot, but before I could speak, he saw me.

"Shale?"

"Daniel."

He stared at me in disbelief.

An awkward moment filled the air between us.

"I thought you were coming," Daniel said at last, "but I dismissed it."

Dr. Luke gazed at me, as if wondering if he should know who I was.

Daniel, realizing his lack of manners, spoke. "Doctor, this is my friend Shale from Brutus Snyder's household, his daughter."

He tipped his head. "Nice to meet you. How is Nathan?"

"Oh, Doctor Luke, he needs Daniel to return."

"Is he sick?"

I couldn't lie to this kind doctor. "No, but he misses Daniel."

Dr. Luke glanced at Daniel.

Daniel shuffled his feet and slicked his curly hair back off his forehead. "I'm sorry to hear that," Daniel mumbled, not making eye contact with me.

The doctor reached over and rubbed Daniel's shoulder in a friendly gesture. "The young woman has traveled far on behalf of Mr. Snyder's son, in a country full of bandits and thieves. You should accompany her back and check on Nathan for her father's sake. The work here will wait until you can return."

I perceived that Daniel felt trapped and angry I had not addressed him privately, but he was too much a gentleman to show it. Of course, he also had a girlfriend, and that meant he would have to leave her behind.

"Yes, Doctor Luke. Of course."

Dr. Luke paused before walking over to his waiting patients. "Give my best to Mister Snyder when you see him."

"Yes, sir. I sure will," I replied.

When Dr. Luke was a respectable distance away, Daniel beseeched me for an answer to the unasked question.

"You can't leave like that, Daniel. Nathan needs you."

"I was fired. Doctor Luke doesn't know it."

"Who fired you?'

"Scylla."

"She can't fire you," I said.

"She can do whatever she wants."

"She's not my mother."

"She's not my mother either, but that doesn't mean I can do whatever I want," Daniel snapped.

He stopped abruptly, glancing around. Our voices were too loud, and a couple of eavesdroppers were listening.

He pointed to a path leading to the back of the inn and motioned for me to go in front of him. "Come."

"Keep going," he prodded me. "There's a table, and we can talk in private."

A few minutes later, we sat face to face, though things weren't the same as before. What was different? That other woman, I felt sure.

"You shouldn't have come." His reprimand was annoying. He looked away from me, refusing to make eye contact.

His elusiveness hurt. "You're treating me...rudely." Even if he was in love with Martha, he could still be nice.

I reached out for his arm, and he pulled it away.

"Don't," he said curtly.

"Fine. Be that way, while Nathan sits in Nazareth crying his heart out because you're gone, and he has no one who understands him or that he can talk to."

"I can't do anything about him," Daniel said tersely.

I shook my head. "Guys are all alike—jerks. I thought you were different. It must be that other woman."

Daniel's eyes grew wide. "What other woman?"

"The one I saw you with when I came into town. You know who I'm talking about."

Daniel seemed perplexed. "No, I don't."

I patted my chest. "I bought this dress from her when I first arrived from the garden. Martha, she sells feminine things—perfumes and such. She has her own booth in town."

"You mean my sister?" Daniel asked.

"That's your sister—Martha? The one you were having a lively conversation with earlier today—who you hugged?"

Daniel laughed. "That's my sister. Back home in my dimension, she runs her own apparel business. She does the same thing here, though on a much smaller scale."

"Martha is your sister?"

"Yes," Daniel said. "Seriously."

I stared at the ground. "I feel foolish."

I detected a softening in his voice. "Shale, the real reason I left isn't because I'm madly in love with another woman, as you're supposing. Scylla demanded that I leave, and when I heard about the arrangement for you to marry Judd, it got complicated."

"How so?"

Daniel crossed his arms pensively. "You don't understand the rules here. You were given to Judd a long time ago. I didn't know. Judd told Scylla it wasn't right I was spending so much time with you, even though we were just friends."

Daniel leaned over the table and whispered. "I don't feel comfortable being around you now. At least not like before."

"Are you crazy? I hate Judd, and he's not even from my dimension."

"When you're with the Romans, you do as the Romans do."

"What's that supposed to mean?"

"It means what it says. You abide by their rules."

"Daniel—"

"What?"

"The real reason I came for you is different. It wasn't because you left me."

"Why did you come, then?"

I inhaled deeply. "After you left, I took the animals on a short day trip over the hills. We ran into a man who lived in the cemetery, half-naked, full of demons, and—"

"And?"

"Let me back up. The reason we went out for the day was because

Judd wasn't feeding the animals. Lowly said he was starving. He wanted to go to a farm some distance away to get food. There wasn't any place close by with pigs."

"There aren't that many pigs in the area because only Gentiles keep them. Pigs are ceremonially unclean and disgusting to Jews."

I sighed. "Later, after the first encounter that terrified me, the wild man darted in and out of the pigs on the hill and sent them scampering. At that moment, a fishing boat pulled up. As the fishermen approached, Cherios said one of the fishermen was the king that I told you about before."

"The lunatic?"

"He's not a lunatic," I corrected.

"Keep going. Get to your point." Daniel glanced behind me.

"You talk about me being impatient—I traveled on the back of a donkey for three hours to get here."

Daniel refocused his eyes on me.

"The wild man ran straight towards the fishermen—the king. The king's eyes stopped him. Demons left the man and went into the pigs. Then the pigs stampeded into the lake and drowned."

"You expect me to believe that?" Daniel asked.

"Yes."

Daniel shook his head. "Shale, I heard a similar story. Gossip travels fast here. You must be exaggerating."

"No. It's true. I wouldn't lie about something like that."

Daniel remained silent for a minute. "So what does that have to do with me, or us?"

I reached for Daniel's arm again. This time he didn't flinch. "I want to take Nathan to see the king. If he could heal that cemetery man, he could help Nathan speak."

Daniel shook his head. "No."

"Look," I continued, "if the king healed Nathan, he could talk and be normal, right? He's not stupid, is he?"

"No." Daniel leaned on the table, propping his chin up on his hand. He gazed past me, as if perceiving something in another world. After a minute, he leaned back with uncharacteristic resignation. "Nothing can heal Nathan. He's been that way since birth."

"What makes you think the king can't heal him?"

"How can I believe something so outlandish? Yes, you saw something that you can't explain, but who knows. Maybe the man wasn't crazy. It could have been staged."

"He tried to attack me on the way over to the farm."

"Maybe that was his practice run before the real thing."

I bit my lower lip. "Why do you say such things?"

"Shale, that man you call the king—he's no healer. He's a charlatan. He's—nothing. He's certainly not a god."

"Suppose you're wrong? Are you going to abandon Nathan without at least trying?"

Daniel stood and began to pace. A couple of minutes passed in silence. I held my breath—and prayed.

Finally, Daniel stopped. "All right, Shale. I'll go back with you and see if we can find this supposed healer, but there's one condition."

"What's that?"

"No one else knows I'm back. And once we've finished our task, proving to you he's a charlatan, I'm coming back here, where I belong."

"Do you hate me for doing this?"

"Do I hate you—for goodness sake, Shale, I don't hate you. You're just—so persistent. And I want to honor the customs of the land in which we find ourselves."

Daniel plopped down on the chair, sighed, and glanced away. "Even if Judd hadn't been chosen for you, I needed to leave."

"How do you think I felt when I found out you were gone without saying good-bye?"

"I wasn't sure. This was arranged in the past before your father married Scylla. In the heat of the moment, I wanted to appease her. I was afraid to consider you—I might make the wrong decision. Perhaps I acted rashly, without considering Nathan's needs. I wish I knew what to do for him."

I fancied if I should confess my love to Daniel—but perhaps it was better to let him wonder. Anyway, he probably knew since he could read my mind. "You will come back with me?"

"Yes, but only with the conditions I gave you."

"Where will you stay?"

"Out of sight." Daniel laughed. "Seriously. You need to find out where that lunatic is hanging out. It won't be easy." He eyed me perceptibly. "How did you get here? I mean, what did you tell Scylla?"

"Nothing. I promised Judd a golden nugget for his help."

"With gold?" Daniel's eyes widened. "I won't ask where that came from."

"I thought you could read my mind," I teased.

"I can, but I have to put effort into it." Daniel leaned forward. "You didn't steal it, did you?"

"Of course not," I said indignantly.

Daniel tugged at his tunic, deep in thought.

I glanced away. I knew he was trying to read my mind.

"So you got it from the garden," he stated.

"Yes."

"*Kol HaKavod.* Well done."

I laughed at his mind-reading ability. I had never told him anything about finding golden nuggets in the garden.

"Why are you looking at me like that?" he asked.

"Nothing. Judd was to tell Scylla I went to search for my father in Jerusalem. She won't expect me back for a few days."

"We'll need to sneak Nathan out of the house. That won't be easy. Nathan never goes anywhere."

"We have time, before Judd wants his golden nugget or thinks I've betrayed him."

"Don't worry about Judd. We've enough to think about taking care of Nathan. Let's go."

We walked to the front of Jacob's Inn to retrieve Baruch. Daniel led the way. Then he paused and touched my arm. "Wait here, Shale, for a second. I need to get something from Doctor Luke. I'll be back in a minute."

"Like what, what do you need?"

"Potion, so Scylla will sleep like a baby." Daniel disappeared inside.

I felt anxious—suppose he meant to leave me here and not come back? Why did I have such doubts? I glanced around. Was there something evil lurking nearby? I sensed something that made me uneasy.

CHAPTER 26

THE ENCHANTER CASTS A SPELL

I stood beside Baruch, rubbing his back.

"You succeeded," Baruch said. "I didn't know how you would get him back."

"Only to take Nathan to the king," I reminded him. "Let's hope the king does more than heal him."

"Like what?" Baruch asked.

"Give me the desires of my heart."

"And what might that be?"

"Lots of things. Just imagine." As we waited for Daniel, I saw something move in the grass—like the last time when we stayed at the inn. The grass was too long to see from so far away. I walked over, curious, to see what it was.

Suddenly, a black snake shot up into the air and flicked his tongue. His flashy eyes caught mine unexpectedly. I tried to turn away from the creature, but the strange tempter hypnotized me. I had never seen a snake behave in such an unusual way. Drumbeats sounded, and the snake began to sway to the music as it increased in intensity.

He called my name. "Shale, my bright and beautiful. I know what you long for, even though you haven't figured it out. I can give it to you."

The creature spoke eloquently, and whispered one word that pierced my heart.

I nodded. "Yes, that's it. Love."

"Oh, Shale, you're so beautiful."

I touched my cheek. "Am I?"

The snake rocked back and forth. Soon more snakes appeared cavorting along with the first one, and the vile creatures turned into handsome men smiling and sending air kisses. Then they changed back into charming snakes attempting to lure me closer.

Baruch whinnied and stomped his hoofs. Why was he doing that?

"Shale, you deserve so much better. Come closer. I can make you feel wonderful. I understand you, Shale, you poor girl who has suffered so."

I couldn't take my eyes off the enchanter. "You understand me?"

The snake danced charmingly. "Do you trust me?"

"I don't know."

"You long to be loved, don't you, sweetheart?"

"Yes, but you're a snake. What do you know about love?"

"I can make it so that you will always feel loved. Would you like that?"

"Yes."

"I can make handsome men desire you."

I sensed something was wrong, but the creature was irresistible. I couldn't turn away. A Gardenia scent, my favorite flower, whisked me to a far-away utopia. Tapping my feet, I swayed my arms to soft melodious strings that kept rhythm with the drums. The serpent, along with its entourage, came closer. The alluring creature spoke pleasant words to me.

So pleasing was the sound of my name. The catcalls entreated me to let myself go free, and the winsome smiles engaged me. Love filled the air as the snake eyes desired me, but another voice spoke.

"Go away," I demanded. "Leave me alone."

I took another step and reached out to touch the sorcerer.

"I'll make you a beautiful princess," he promised.

The desire to be talented and sought after by handsome young men consumed me.

Footsteps approached, and a familiar voice addressed me. "Shale, come to me."

Daniel was too late. I didn't want him anymore. I laughed.

"Shale, come to me." The snake used the same words as Daniel. I stared into the depths of the creature's eyes, and evil pricked my soul.

"Give me your hand, Shale, now," Daniel demanded. "I'm going to pull you towards me."

I reached back, and Daniel's hand clasped mine. Tugging at me, he drew me towards him. I wanted to jerk my hand away. The snake still held me within its clutches, hypnotizing me, refusing to let me go.

"Shale, look at me," Daniel urged.

The snake persisted. "I can give you everything you want."

I felt trapped between the two—why was it so difficult to choose? Suddenly a white dove passed overhead. The unexpected movement surprised me, enough to break the spell. I collapsed in Daniel's arms, burying my face in his chest.

Daniel wrapped his arms around me. "You're okay, thank goodness. I felt you might be in danger, and when Baruch whinnied, I came out to see. Next time I won't delay."

Several men nearby shouted for help and hurried over to see the black cobra. A commotion ensued, though I was too afraid to watch them kill it.

I had witnessed that darkness before. Now I knew what it was. The serpent reminded me of the cartoon characters that covered my bedroom walls, the king's temptation in the wilderness, the snake that slithered through my hand in the garden, the wiggly shapes the vultures chased, and the vile creatures that entered the pigs.

I exhaled. The darkness still invaded my mind and filled me with terrifying images. I feared fear itself, the worst kind of darkness, but I would soon learn this was just the beginning of the battle for my soul.

CHAPTER 27

T HE SHEEP

As we headed back to my father's villa in Galilee, I didn't want to talk about what happened. Although Daniel left me alone to sort it out and his presence walking beside me was reassuring, I couldn't share with him my innermost struggle. Why did I have this feeling that something evil wanted me?

Upon returning, we stopped beside the road a couple of hundred furlongs from my father's estate. Here we got into a heated discussion about how to get Nathan out of the house that night.

"I think you should have Worldly Crow create a distraction with Mari, and you put the potion in her wine," Daniel insisted. "After all, he's good at causing diversions."

"Mari promised me she would do anything to help me, and I don't trust Worldly Crow. I don't trust any crow."

We were at an impasse. To get this far and disagree on such an important detail upset me.

Daniel inspected the potion in the flask and gently shook it. "You get one chance to get this right. Scylla would be furious if she knew you were doing this."

"I know. Mari cares about Nathan. Knowing we're taking him to be healed will motivate her to go along with us."

Daniel listened but appeared unconvinced.

"It's better that Mari help us rather than try to sneak Nathan out— as long as we're back by the time Scylla wakes up. Did you find out where the king is?"

"Me?" Daniel asked.

"Yes."

"The fisherman, you mean?" Daniel set the flask down and leaned back, propping himself up on his elbows as he admired the field. The sun had dipped behind the trees on the horizon. "I refuse to call him a king."

The way Daniel said it, he was adamant.

"Fine—the healer," I said reluctantly.

Daniel rolled his eyes. "Whatever."

The reddish glow on Daniel's tan face and brown hair made him appear even more handsome than usual.

"You better go and tell her," Daniel said. "I'm anxious to get started. May God grant us success."

I stood and brushed the dirt from my dress. "Wish me luck."

Daniel handed me the potion. "No, not luck. I'll be praying."

"Thanks." I smiled and headed up the road towards my father's house. The evening sun had sunk below the green fields and dusty road. The air was heavy with humidity. Some doves cooed from the trees, and a flock of sheep grazed on the hill.

Did Daniel ever say if he knew where the king was? I should have asked when we were in town, but the cobra encounter befuddled my thinking.

I listened from the corner of the house for Mari—rattling of dishes, shaking out the rugs, even her voice. Not hearing anything, I stole around to the other side. She was lugging water from the well. That was my chore, but since I wasn't here, she had to do my job, too. She was too visible for me to run and greet. Scylla or Judd might see me. I'd wait until she was closer.

A few minutes later, I whispered to her. Mari stopped abruptly and looked around.

"Mari, it's Shale, over here."

She grinned. "Shale, you're back."

"Come here and act normal. You never saw me, okay?"

"Okay." Mari looked perplexed but glad to see me.

"Set the water down, and I'll explain."

"Sure."

I told Mari the details of our plan. "Put this medicine in Scylla's wine tonight. It will make her very sleepy. Daniel and I want to take Nathan to be healed by the king—the teacher who is performing miracles, but Scylla wouldn't let us if she knew. We'll get Nathan as soon as she's asleep and leave. We should be back before she wakes up. Can you help us?"

Mari nodded. "I'll do it for Nathan."

"Awesome." I reached over and gave her hug. "Here, take this."

Mari examined the flask and smelled the mixture. "What is it?"

"It's a sedative—will make her fall asleep."

"Okay. I'll give it to her."

"Good. Now, I need a sign to know that you've put the medicine in Scylla's drink, and she has drunk it. What can we use?"

"I could sing a song."

"Yes, that's it. Sing that song you sang to me when I was sick with fever. Then Daniel and I will know she's asleep, and it's safe to sneak inside."

"Yes, ma'am." Mari tucked the sleep medicine inside the top of her dress. "You might want to get him right away."

I nodded. "I'll be close by," I assured her. "The sooner, the better. Thanks again."

"You're welcome." Mari walked back to pick up the bucket, and I waved to her as she threw me a kiss.

I hurried back down the street to let Daniel know everything was set.

"Where are we going?" he asked.

"I thought you found out where to go."

"No. I had to get the medicine from Doctor Luke, the potion."

I bit my lip. I was always great with ideas but not so much with the details. "How do we know where to go if we don't know where the king is?"

Daniel ignored my king reference. "That's for you to figure out. This is your adventure, Shale."

"But you're a guy. It seems more natural for you to ask the men than for me." I went and sat on a log by Baruch, crossing my arms and fretting. Men could be so stubborn.

A sweet sound interrupted my complaining spirit. I glanced up and saw Much-Afraid sprinting across the pasture. She greeted me with cheerful yips.

"How did you get here?"

"I dug a hole underneath the fence. Hadn't seen you all day."

I scratched her behind the ear as she wiggled.

Daniel asked again, "What do you want to do? I thought you knew where he was. Why didn't you ask me earlier?"

"I did."

"No, you didn't."

A couple of minutes passed as we stared at each other. It was too late to go anywhere, and there wasn't a soul nearby who would know anything about an itinerant preacher or healer.

Soon a sheep approached us from the flock in the nearby field. Sheep never traveled alone because they need a shepherd to guide them. Daniel eyed the sheep curiously.

When the sheep got close enough, he spoke. "Shale, I'm Little."

"Little?"

"You know me."

"Yes, that's right. You took Baruch to meet the king."

The sheep nodded. "Anyone who cries out, I will answer him. Someday people will see the king's spirit in extraordinary people like Martin Luther, David Livingstone, Corrie Ten Boom, and Hudson Taylor. Today I humbly do the king's bidding for you. I'm a sheep, like so many others, listening and obeying the great shepherd's voice."

I glanced behind the sheep and saw the dozens of sheep on the hill. Why was this sheep called out from all the others?

The sheep answered me without asking. "I was chosen to bring you this message."

Daniel asked, "Shale, who are you talking to?"

I held up my hand for him to be quiet.

The sheep continued. "Go to the Sea of Galilee and into the region of the Decapolis in the morning, and he'll be there to receive you. Peace is with you, my child." The sheep turned back in the direction from which he came.

Daniel watched the sheep disappear before saying anything. "Don't tell me you were talking to that sheep."

"I was."

He rolled his eyes. "How do you do that? I didn't hear anything."

"Like you can talk to Nathan and I can't."

Daniel stared silently at me for a long time before speaking. "So what did the sheep tell you? Or do I even need to ask?"

"You know."

"Yes," Daniel said. "We're leaving for the Decapolis with Nathan."

"Let's not wait until the morning." I stood. "I'm going back to the house to listen for Mari's singing."

Daniel nodded. "I'll stay here with Baruch."

"Come," I said to Much-Afraid. "You can keep me company while I wait."

CHAPTER 28

T HE HEALING

Hours later, Mari's melodic voice floated on a gentle breeze. I had fought hard not to fall asleep. I scrambled back to Daniel who lay on the grass half-awake. "Scylla is asleep. We can get Nathan anytime."

Daniel yawned. "Great. Let's get a few hours' rest, and we'll sneak him out in the morning."

"No, don't wait. Who knows how long the sedative will last."

"You want me to go right now?"

"Yes."

Daniel reluctantly got up and rubbed his eyes. With his athletic build silhouetted against the moonlight, could anything foil him? He looked too strong.

"I'll walk over with you and wait," I offered.

"Are you sure you want to do this?" Daniel asked.

"Of course I'm sure." We had to before he changed his mind. I couldn't bear that we had come this far and not succeed. Just meeting the king again was enough to compel me not to chicken out.

A few minutes later, Daniel and I stood out front. Daniel nodded— as if asking me to pray for him or wish him luck. I did both. He disappeared into the house, and I crouched down in the leaves, listening for anything, whether good or bad. The time ticked too slowly. I blew on my hands and rubbed them together to keep me awake and shoo away the butterflies in my stomach.

Several minutes later, Nathan and Daniel walked through the front door. I sprang from my hiding place. No one else could have snuck Nathan out so quietly. Daniel had draped his arm on Nathan's shoulder to guide him as he stumbled in the dark. Soon we made it to the street. I breathed heavily, releasing pent-up tension.

"Ca-Ca. Where are you going, Shale?" Worldly Crow had found us, and as usual, had come at the worst possible moment.

"We're going to see the king," I replied. "Shhhh."

"What?" Daniel asked.

"I'm talking to Worldly Crow."

"Worldly Crow?" Daniel glanced back at the black bird now following us. He shrugged. "Whatever."

We headed back to our hiding place and prepared to leave. I sent Much-Afraid to the cave, so it was just Baruch and us.

The first hour passed in silence. Nathan and Daniel walked beside me as I rode. Daniel took a few moments and explained to Nathan about the king and my desire to see him healed. Nathan thanked me with his eyes.

We passed through the region of Tyre and Sidon. We approached the Sea of Galilee at dawn, and a little later entered the Decapolis, where we came upon a throng of people gathered on a hillside. I stood on my tippy toes to get a view, but I couldn't see towards the front.

"We'll need to leave Baruch here and walk down," I told Daniel.

Baruch heehawed. "I want to see the king, too."

"Sorry, Baruch, not this time. You had lots of time with the king in the garden. This is Nathan's moment."

Baruch hung his head, "Yes, Miss Shale. You're right."

I patted Baruch on the nose and tethered him underneath a shade tree.

Daniel guided Nathan in front of him, and we squeezed our way in among the crowds. I recognized the fishermen who had been with the king in Gadara when he cast out the demons.

One came up and asked us. "What do you need?"

Daniel replied, "We have a young mute man with us who needs healing."

The man waved his hand at the crowds amassed on the hill. "The master is busy right now. Can't you see?"

Sometimes my persistence, though annoying to some, paid off. "Please let us take Nathan to the healer. We have come a long ways."

I glanced behind him. We had gotten the king's attention. I pleaded, "If the teacher could touch Nathan, I know he would heal him."

The man left to speak privately with the king.

A couple of minutes later, the king walked up and greeted us. His eyes showed tenderness and concern. "Follow me."

The king guided us away from the people to a secluded spot. He showed Nathan where to sit. After praying, the king spat onto his hand and touched Nathan's tongue. Looking up to heaven, he cried, "Ephphatha!"

Nathan opened his mouth wide and moved his tongue for the first time. His eyes grew bright. Laughing, he turned to the king. Speaking plainly, he talked with an exuberance that amazed me.

Nathan bowed on his knees before the healer, uttering praises. "Thank you, my Lord, for healing me."

Then he turned to the rest of us. "I can speak. I can speak. Hear me." He reached over to Daniel and shook him. "I can speak. Can you hear me?"

Daniel nodded.

Nathan bowed before the king once more. "Thank you, Lord."

The king said, "When you leave here, don't tell anyone what I've done."

By this time, the crowds had followed us. The people looked on in amazement. Many shook their heads in disbelief.

"Who is this man that does such miracles? Where does he come from?" they asked.

"He comes from Nazareth," one follower responded.

"Nazareth—can anything good come from there?"

The healer had brought division to the people. Daniel watched with interest. I noticed that he and the king exchanged glances. Daniel's nod towards the king filled me with hope. How long would it be before he understood?

The king's eyes pierced the darkness of my heart, but I did not feel judged. Goose bumps crept up my arms. Ecstasy overflowed. Joy I had not known flowed through me in a way I didn't understand. Words weren't necessary.

The king knew my innermost imperfections but covered my flaws with his perfection. I slipped down and sat at his feet. He placed his hand on my head and prayed, speaking to me softly.

"I love you, Shale, more than you will know. Don't let anyone steal your joy. There's no one else like you. Believe."

I sobbed as I sat in a crumbled heap. I didn't want what happened between us to end. I was changed, but I didn't know how or what it meant. One thing I did know—I wanted to be a daughter of the king.

Nathan continued walking among the crowds, sharing his healing. The amazement of the crowds grew. "He has done everything well," they said. "He even makes the deaf hear and the mute speak."

Daniel kept his eyes on the king. I could perceive the wheels of belief churning in his intellectual mind. He needed more time. The king smiled at me once more as we prepared to leave.

I longed to know him deeply. How could one person be so awesome, so perfect, and so loving? I knew he was more than just an ordinary man. He had to be who he said he was.

We had almost made it back up the hill when I saw the beggar from Dothan. As he raised his hands towards the heavens, joy overflowed. I rushed up to him, and he stopped worshiping to acknowledge me. A questioning look crossed his face.

"You are healed," I exclaimed.

The man touched his eyes and then thrust his hands into the sky. "The king healed me. I can see!"

"That's wonderful. Then you know the king, too," I said excitedly.

The man reached for my hand and squeezed it, as he had done long ago. He smiled broadly. "You gave me a coin once, when I was blind."

"Yes, I did. And you prayed for me to receive a blessing."

We stood for a moment, hands locked, and then he let me go. I smiled at him as I walked away.

Daniel called to me, from higher up the hill.

A few minutes later, I climbed on Baruch's back and readied myself as an ole pro now in donkey riding, but sadness filled my heart. We had to leave too soon. I wanted to savor the memory so it would last forever. And Fifi—I knew he was safe. I had peace. The king's eyes— they pierced my soul and loved me anyway.

"Shale, are you okay?"

Daniel's voice jolted me back to reality.

"Yes." I sat quietly for a minute before continuing. "He's the king above all kings."

"You think so?" Daniel was walking alongside Baruch as I sat on the donkey.

"And you don't?"

Daniel pursed his lips. "I don't know what to think."

Worldly Crow landed on a palm tree as we passed by. "That was spectacular. Some kind of magic, uh? How did he learn how to do that?"

"He didn't learn, Worldly Crow."

"What's that?" Daniel glanced at me.

I chuckled. "Oh, Worldly Crow called the healer a magician."

Daniel grinned. "That's a thought."

I turned to Nathan. "What's the first thing you're going to say to Scylla when we return?"

Nathan's eyes were fixated on the ground. He murmured. "I'm not going to say anything."

"What? Tell me you're kidding. You're healed, and you're not going to share with others what the king did for you?"

"Didn't he tell me not to tell anyone?"

I rolled my eyes. "I don't think that's what he meant, Nathan. Really."

"Then what did he mean when he told me not to tell anyone?"

"I don't know. Maybe don't tell people until they are ready to listen."

"I'll reveal what the king has done, but only to my father. I want him to hear me first."

I stared at Nathan. "You mean we brought you all the way out here, risking the wrath of Scylla sneaking you out, and you aren't even going to speak to her?"

"Besides," Nathan continued. "I want Daniel to remain with us and not leave. That won't happen if Scylla knows I can talk."

"Nathan," Daniel scolded, "you can't manipulate people like that. I go where I want. No one controls me, not even you."

My heart sank. This was not turning out the way I wanted. Already my joy was evaporating. I was still stuck with an evil stepmother, an absent father, betrothed to a man I hated, and the one I wanted to be with was leaving. Anger crept into my thoughts. My good intentions to heal Nathan had not accomplished everything I had hoped for, and yet, the king's smile still glowed in my mind, and his voice lingered in my ears, "Don't let others steal your joy."

Worldly Crow cackled. "Ca-Ca. I've come from Jerusalem. Many religious leaders say that man is a fraud."

"What do you know about anything, Worldly Crow? Go away. Let me be."

With that, the crow took off in a huff, leaving me to ponder all these things in my heart.

CHAPTER 29

SECRETS REVEALED

We were gone longer than I meant to be, arriving late in the afternoon. Daniel wanted to leave, but I coaxed him to put Baruch in the cave and Nathan in the house. Nathan was determined to continue as a mute young man in the Snyder household.

We were crossing the veranda in the portico when Scylla spotted us. She stood as a statue with hands anchored on both hips. Her malignant eyes rested on me. Even though we were still a good distance away, none of us could escape her toxic wrath.

"This isn't going to be good," Nathan said.

Judd stood under a palm tree. His mouth gaped when Nathan spoke, but I was too startled to think about him. As Scarlet said in *Gone With the Wind*, I'll think about that tomorrow.

When we were within earshot, Scylla started in on me.

"Shale, where have you been? You didn't even tell Mari where you were. I've been worried sick about Nathan."

Daniel took Nathan inside the house. I felt exposed and defense-less. Why did Daniel depart so abruptly?

"We took Nathan to the healer."

Scylla frowned. "What healer."

"The king. Some call him master."

Scylla glared. "It's because of him that your father is stuck in Jerusalem. That 'miracle worker' has usurped the Roman government, and the religious establishment hates him." Scylla scoffed. "He's a Jew, and yet the council despises him. What does that tell you? Another John the Baptist—I hear he was beheaded."

She rolled her eyes. "How can you be so gullible, Shale? So-called healers are a dime a dozen here. They stand on street corners and steal your money. A bunch of charlatans, they are. If Doctor Luke couldn't heal Nathan, no one can. For Nathan's sake, I'll go easy on Daniel."

"You lied to me," I said.

Scylla shook her finger at me. "Don't ever accuse me of lying."

"What you told me was a lie."

"I didn't lie to you."

Footsteps approached from behind, but I kept my eyes on Scylla. "What did Judd tell you about Daniel and me?"

She glared, furious she couldn't control me.

The porch door opened and Daniel emerged. He stood tentatively studying the developing situation.

"Go ahead. While you're at it, tell us what you told Daniel."

Scylla thrust her pointed nose into the air. "How dare you to speak to me that way." "No matter. You are what you are."

She turned to Judd. "Lock her up in her private quarters so she can't go on any more escapades."

Judd hesitated.

"Do it now!" she ordered.

Scylla reminded me of a vulture with bulging eyes—her long spindly neck and pointed nose could only be a weak man's trophy. I hated that she was my father's prize.

"I want my money," Judd whispered.

"Wait," Nathan shouted. A voice never heard on my father's estate filled the portico. He edged his way around Daniel and proceeded to walk towards Scylla.

She gasped and covered her heart. "You—you can talk!"

"I've heard it all," Nathan said. "Scylla, you're a deceptive, conniving, vindictive woman. You don't care about Shale or me."

Her eyes boiled with anger. "That's not true."

"Be quiet," Nathan demanded.

No one said a word or moved, too shocked at hearing Nathan's voice.

"Do you know what it's like to be mute and unable to utter a single word? You spoke constant lies, and I couldn't do anything about it."

Scylla glared at Nathan.

Nathan turned to Daniel. "You've been my friend for the last three and a half years—a good friend. I love you Daniel."

Daniel lowered his eyes, embarrassed by the straightforwardness of Nathan's expression of gratitude.

"But how can you deny what the king did for me?"

Daniel stared at the ground, appearing emotional and conflicted. "I'm not denying it," corrected Daniel. "I'm just slow to believe."

Nathan turned to Judd. "You're wicked."

"Who made you the man of the house?" crooned Scylla.

Nathan ignored her question. "I want my father to come home."

Scylla shook her head. "No."

"Why not?" I asked. "So you can continue to torture and control the rest of us."

"I think I should leave," Daniel said. "This is a family matter."

"No, come back," I pleaded. "If you care anything about me."

Daniel stopped. His eyes appeared torn between pity and anger.

Dark clouds formed over us, casting shadows around the portico. The wind picked up as if a storm were approaching.

"Shale is right," Daniel said. "I shouldn't leave until everything is resolved. Maybe that's why I'm here."

"We don't need you anymore, Daniel," Scylla retorted.

"Even though I can talk, I don't want Daniel to leave," Nathan insisted. "He's done nothing wrong."

"He's no longer needed unless you want to waste your inheritance."

"Mine or yours?" Nathan questioned.

Scylla didn't respond.

Nathan said, "You've made my father weak, a shell of a man. He didn't used to be that way. You ruined him. He works all the time. Lies, lies, and more lies. You want his money—your god."

Scylla stood frozen as ice, probably too stunned to speak.

"Not only that," Nathan continued, "but you've lied repeatedly. What Judd said to you isn't what you told Shale."

"So the truth comes out," I scoffed.

Scylla recovered quickly, now simmering near the boiling point. She turned from Nathan and pointed her finger at Judd. "I told you to take Shale to her room. Lock her up. She's still alive because of me. I'll speak to you later."

She turned back to Nathan. "You might not be mute anymore, but you're still dumb. You don't know what you're talking about."

Judd pushed me ahead.

"Stop," I fired back.

He prodded me again. "Then move."

I looked pleadingly at Daniel. He could stand up to Scylla, but would he? How could she exert so much control over men? Daniel followed me with his eyes as I walked past but remained quiet. I was disappointed he didn't put a halt to Scylla's reckless accusations.

We climbed the stairs to my room, and a veil of darkness shrouded me. Fifi's dead body appeared once again in a vision at the bottom of the stairs. I had hoped the memory wouldn't torture me anymore. Why hadn't the king healed me? I grabbed the post to catch my balance. Rain started to fall.

"What's wrong with you?"

"Nothing."

"I want my money."

"Give me a second, will you?"

Judd opened the door. I went over to my bed feeling in the blankets for the rocks.

I handed him a golden nugget. "Here."

Judd grimaced, dropping the rock. The nugget rolled on the floor.

"What's wrong?" I reached down and picked it up. The nugget sizzled in my hand but felt cool to the touch. Judd clutched his burnt fingers.

"Let me see," I demanded.

When he opened up his clasped fingers, fiery welts scoured his palm. The rock glowed as I held it, but it didn't burn me.

Judd cradled his hand. "I don't want your rock. Could your king heal even this?" He shoved his seared hand towards me. His voice was bitter.

I briefly felt sorry for Judd, but it was easier to hate him. I didn't want to admit it, but the more I hated him, the worse I felt. A fit of depression closed in on me.

"So that king of yours did heal Nathan." Judd said it as a statement rather than a question. "Maybe there's something to him after all."

"That's for you to find out." Would the king do anything for Judd? In my smugness, a voice pricked my soul. "What about the healed man in the cemetery?"

He stormed out clutching his hand and locking the door from the outside. I felt as if I were a wounded bird in a cage. Could I still hear the king's voice in my pain? The voice wasn't as loud in my heart, but I still heard it. "Don't let others steal your joy."

What joy could I have stuck here behind a locked door? I stared at the ceiling. If I didn't write in my diary, I would explode.

I got up from my bed and grabbed the reed-pen and paper.

"Dear Dog, if ever you were real, can you show yourself to me now, before I wilt from sadness? I've done a good thing, and yet I'm being punished for it. Where is justice? Why can't the king's love reach me? I'm feel as if I'm a wounded bird, stuck in a cage where I don't belong."

. . .

I thought for a moment before writing more.

"I must be sure. Are you and the king the same? He seems like a father to me. Can you heal me? You seem so far away."

CHAPTER 30

T
HE VISITOR

Several hours had passed when footsteps pounded the stony stairs outside. I ran over and peered through the small crack in the door. It was Mari. Thank goodness for her or I'd die stuck in this room. I sat on the bed while she unlocked the door.

"What's happening downstairs?" I asked.

Mari set the tray of food beside me. "Good things."

"What good things?" I picked up a piece of bread, broke it in two, and took a bite. I wasn't hungry, but thought I should eat while I could.

"Daniel took Nathan to Jerusalem so your father could see that his son is healed."

"That's great. I'm glad Daniel did that for Nathan. How long will it be before they return?"

Mari smiled. "It's hard to say. I suppose they could be gone for several months."

"Several months? That's ridiculous."

"Why are you always in such a hurry, my love?"

"What am I going to do here while I wait?" Not to see Daniel for that long would be torture. To be stuck here with Judd and Scylla was unimaginable.

Mari looked at me perceptibly. "Are you feeling okay?"

"I suppose. Just depressed."

"I understand."

"When can I get out of here? I mean, she can't keep me locked up forever."

"Oh, she won't," Mari assured me. "She wants to protect you."

"Protect me?"

"She doesn't want you to get hurt."

I snorted. "Did you hear how she talked to me?"

"Oh, she didn't mean it, my love. She was just angry."

"Sure she didn't mean it. Are you blind or something?"

Mari shook her head. "But you traipse off. There are robbers and murderers out there."

"Daniel was with me. Anyway, I'm done eating."

Mari looked at the tray of uneaten food. "Are you sure?"

"Yes."

"I'll come back in the morning and check on you."

"Can you do me another favor?"

"What's that, my love?"

"Check on the animals for me. Make sure Judd is taking care of Lowly, Much-Afraid, and Cherios. How I wish I could visit them."

Mari stared at the floor.

"It's okay. I know you would get in trouble if you let me out of here. That's why I want you to check on them for me."

"Sure. I will," Mari promised.

Later that night as I sat on my bed, the sound of feet alarmed me again. I never had anyone visit after dark. The door unlatched. I held my breath. Scylla strutted in. I never thought I'd be happy to see her in my room.

Her words were slurred. "You've no idea the trouble you've caused me."

I stared at her.

"Your father and I were doing your mother a favor taking you in."

"It's not as if she asked me."

"There's nothing you can do to pull us apart, try as you might."

"I haven't done anything."

"Why did you say those things about me this afternoon? The world isn't all about you, Shale Snyder."

How could one person have so many different moods? She was like a cat with nine lives—nice one minute and spiteful the next, except I had ended up with the jealous cat life.

"Why don't you answer my question, why did you say what you did about Daniel and me?"

"I assumed because you were spending so much time alone with him."

"It wasn't that much," I muttered.

"You aren't as smart as you think you are. Even if you were brilliant, you should credit it to your father, which you seem reluctant to do. Your mother is unfit to be your mother."

I balled my hand under the blanket into a fist. Too bad I couldn't throw a book at her, but they weren't yet invented.

"I've heard all about her," Scylla continued. "And you're just like her."

"What gall you have to make such accusations."

"I'll stand by your father and defend him in every way I can."

"Fine," I said. "Kudos to him."

"Your mother and father have deceived you," she continued. "Your stepfather, that is. Brutus sent you wonderful gifts. Don't you know they broke them?"

"That's not true," I argued. "I opened all of them. Some of them Remi tried to fix, after they got married."

"You couldn't remember that. You were too young."

"They just got married. I gave him the one from last year." What was the use? I studied the blanket on my bed. I used all the self-control I could muster to hold back saying something I might regret later.

We existed in different worlds. Who was in the real world, her or me? Did my father even love me? Scylla had no way of knowing about the broken gifts unless he told her. I rubbed the egg in my dress pocket underneath the blanket.

"What are you thinking?" Scylla asked. "Speak to me."

"Why? You don't like me, you don't believe anything I say, and you make up stories about me that aren't true." I turned my back to her.

"You're right," Scylla said. "And you will pay for it. I control everything having to do with your father. I speak for him and write his letters. He's very busy."

She tossed her head defiantly and strutted to the door. "I can even make it so you don't see him again." She yanked the door behind her.

Did I want to know the truth? Maybe it was all too painful. What was Scylla's motive for coming to see me—to hurt me, to make me hate my mother and stepfather? Maybe my father left because of something she said about me. Maybe that's why he didn't come back. I didn't trust her. I reached for my reed-pen and started writing.

"Help me, king of the garden, to know the answers."

CHAPTER 31

S OJOURN OF THE AGES

Several days went by that were much the same as the day before. I was stuck with nothing to do but dream—and write. Dream of better times, of being home again—which at times I sorely missed—and at other moments, I felt sorry for myself. I wanted to see Daniel. When would Nathan and my father return, if ever?

"Ruff."

Much-Afraid was making her daily rounds.

I climbed up to the tiny window and looked out. "Hi, Much-Afraid."

The dog was several feet below me, ready to play if I could come outside. "How much longer are you going to be stuck in there?"

I sighed. "I guess until my father comes back." I twisted the ends of my hair, which had become quite long. "How are Lowly and Cherios?"

"They are doing fine. And guess what?"

"What?"

"Judd is feeding us the best oats now."

"I'm glad to hear that." That was a dramatic change for the better. I leaned out over the window. "Can you do me a favor?"

Much-Afraid wagged her tail. "What's that?"

"Do you ever see Worldly Crow around?"

"When he's here. He travels the countryside a lot."

"Next time you see him, tell him I want him to do something for me."

Much-Afraid barked a few times. "Okay."

"How is Baruch?"

"He's doing great, except he complains about not having any apples."

I rubbed my tongue over my teeth. Wished that were my only worry. "Don't forget to tell Worldly Crow."

"He was here yesterday. I'll look for him," Much-Afraid said.

"What's Cherios up to?"

Much-Afraid chased her tail for a few seconds before answering. "She tells us many stories about the king and keeps us entertained. The other animals have become quite fond of her."

"That's cool. I'm glad she's been well received."

Much-Afraid swatted at a fly. "Let me go find Worldly Crow for you."

"Is Lowly getting fed, too?" I asked.

"He's getting fed what seems good to him, although I wouldn't eat it. Pigs aren't so choosy, though."

I laughed. "I'll see you soon."

"I don't think you'll be stuck in there much longer. You'll figure out a way to escape."

"I hope."

Much-Afraid took off towards the front. Pressed up against the wall, I slid down from the window. The warm sunlight filtered in through the window giving me hope that Much-Afraid was right.

A short time later, I received a visitor. Worldly Crow landed on the windowsill, cackling at me impatiently. "*Ca-ca.*"

He shook his feathers, and dust particles floated in the filtered light.

"What did you want to see me for, Shale?"

I was lying on my bed daydreaming and rose when I heard his cackles. "Worldly Crow, thanks for coming. I need to ask you for a favor."

He cocked his head sideways. "What's that?"

"I want you to get the key to the door and unlock it for me so I can get out of here."

Worldly Crow cackled. "You want me to sneak into the house and find the key, and then come back and unlock the door?"

"Worldly Crow, if you can steal a fish from a crowded marketplace, you can steal a key from Mari."

"When do you want me to do this?"

"Right now. Today." I slouched back on my bed. "I'm going to go insane if I don't get out of here." I shuffled my feet impatiently. "Have you seen the king anywhere?"

"Yes, he has remained close by—in the Decapolis."

My depressed mood perked up upon hearing this good news. "Please go do it now, quickly."

"As you wish, but it's not an easy thing for a crow to sneak into the house undetected. For one thing, I've got to get the door open."

I studied Worldly Crow. "You can do it, I have confidence in you." I flitted my hand at him. "Go."

A short time later, wings fluttered outside nearby. I jumped up to the window in time to see the crow strut up to the door. I scrambled over and looked through the peephole. He held the key in his beak and attempted to put it into the keyhole, but it fell out. Worldly Crow mumbled under his breath and picked it up again.

"You can stick it in there. Try again."

It took two more times, but he unlocked the door.

"You're brilliant, my friend."

"It wasn't so easy as you made it out to be. What are you going to do now?"

"Go tell Baruch, Much-Afraid, Lowly, and Cherios to rendezvous with me at our old hideout. We're going on a journey."

"Where?"

"To see the king."

"Again?"

"When I'm with him, he fills me with hope. I want to see him again. Who knows—maybe I won't come back here."

"Things could be worse. You aren't starving. You have a roof over your head. You have Mari and me and all the other animals."

"I don't need a lecture. Go get the animals, and tell them to meet me. Hurry."

"You're the most impatient girl I've ever met."

"Go."

I grabbed the ceramic egg and the two golden rocks and put them in my pocket. I stopped and thought about my diary. I had to leave it. I had no place to put it. When I exited the stairs, I almost fainted. Mari saw me and started to say something, but I covered my mouth with my finger. She stopped, smiled faintly, and waved. I took it to mean, see you soon.

I hurried to our old hideout and waited. It didn't take long for my animal friends to get wind of our trip, and I greeted them on the dirt road. Much-Afraid trotted up to me, and I squatted down to hug her.

"How did you get out without Judd seeing you?"

"He wasn't around. He left earlier today to go somewhere," Baruch said.

"Good."

Baruch asked. "Where are we headed, Miss Shale?"

"To the Decapolis."

"That's where we went before."

"Worldly Crow said the king is in the same general area."

"Look for the crowds," Baruch said.

Cherios hopped from rock to rock, singing praises to the king as if she were in the garden. Lowly and Much-Afraid played dog and pig games.

Soon we were joined by a woman on a donkey with a small child. "Where are you headed?" she asked.

"We're on our way to the Decapolis to meet the king."

"So am I," the woman said. "My baby needs healing."

I glanced down at the little one she held in her arms. "Let's travel together."

She nodded. We rode for a while beside each other. Two more joined us. As we walked, one of the men said, "We heard the king is in the Decapolis. We want to meet him."

"That's where we're going, too." Our small caravan grew larger as we walked.

Three more joined us, then five, ten, twenty. The road opened wide, and dozens more joined our band. Some came in robes, others in gowns, still others in uniforms and ordinary clothes from every country. Some were rich and some were poor. Some were old and some were young. Some were famous and some not so famous. Some lived at that time and others were yet to be born—all traveling on the same road to meet the king. The sheep, Little, joined us. We were as a flock in search of a shepherd.

Before my eyes, the heavens opened. Thousands of angels walked alongside us. More angels flew overhead, gleaming swords in hand, protecting us from wicked demons in pursuit of wanderers and lost souls who weren't yet claimed. The angels were stronger.

Warriors shouted prayers and fighters waged a valiant defense against usurpers and underlings and demons and all who sought to kill the king's possessions. For the first time in my life, I knew I had become part of a great battle. I was not just Shale Snyder. I was a daughter of the king worth fighting for—even unto death.

On all sides, throngs of people watched the great spectacle. I wasn't walking alone. In fact, I'd never been alone. Even hiding in the closet long ago, I wasn't alone. Thunderous shouts and clapping hands shook the heavens. The clanging of swords echoed, creating sparks in the sky like firecrackers. Thousands of dark underlings fell from the heavens like battered hail.

We sang as we traveled. *"Hineh ma tov 'mana'yim, shevet achim gam yachad.* Behold, how good and how pleasant it is for brothers to dwell together."

It didn't take long to find the crowd—over four thousand souls gathered before the king.

CHAPTER 32

U NEXPECTED ENCOUNTER

Much-Afraid plopped down in the grass, and Cherios sat in my lap. The seekers gathered in small groups, sitting on flat rocks, grass, and blankets. The king walked among us, picking up small children and blessing them. His voice reached even me, so far away, words of encouragement, peace, and love. Nothing could deafen his voice to those who wished to hear him.

Hours went by, but the moments passed too quickly. I listened, mesmerized, hanging on to every word as if it might be his last. My heart marveled with the rest of the crowd at his teachings.

Much-Afraid snuggled up to me, and Cherios cleaned her paws. Her eyes were bright in the king's presence, as if she were home in the garden. Baruch munched on the grass. After months of worry that he would be turned into bacon, Lowly made a surprise announcement, "The king loves me, even a lowly pig like me."

The king spoke with authority unlike anyone had spoken to me before.

"Come unto me, all of you that labor and are heavy laden, and I will give you rest. Take my yoke upon you, and learn from me; for I am meek and lowly in heart, and you will find rest for your souls. For my yoke is easy, and my burden is light."

"How can he know so much, being a carpenter from Galilee?" one man remarked.

"I think he's John the Baptist," another man said.

"I think he's Elijah," a woman countered.

"I believe he's the Son of God," I announced to the others.

After a while, the king took a break to discuss some business with his disciples. Soon baskets were passed around stacked with fish and bread.

"Where did the fish come from?" someone asked.

People shook their heads. No one knew. "We're so remote here, there's no bread or fish for miles," a woman muttered.

I waited for a basket. A boy with a shawl covering his eyes approached and offered me a helping.

I glanced up at the boy's face and almost fainted. "Judd?"

"He nodded and smiled in a strange sort of way.

What was he doing here? I glanced down at his hand. It was healed. Others were waiting for me to take my portion. I reached in and took some fish and bread, watching as he continued to the next person.

"How can that be?" I asked.

"I told you, Shale, he has been feeding us better," Much-Afraid said.

"Why would the king want to heal him?" My life hadn't changed. What about me? A voice spoke to me. "Don't let others steal your joy. Don't be jealous of others or concerned about not receiving their blessing. Think about the good things the king has given you."

I didn't want to deny what the king said, but I also wasn't willing to believe Judd was worth healing. I knew my attitude was wrong, but in my anger, I couldn't change what I felt.

I hated Judd—since I was twelve, and he put the curse on me. Who wouldn't hate him? No matter how hard I tried, though, I was unable to justify my own stinking selfishness.

Evening came. I wanted to love, but I was unwilling to give up my hate. Could the king's words penetrate my hardened heart? What joy would fill me if I surrendered everything to the king?

Baruch nudged me with his nose. "Where do we go now, Miss Shale?"

The crowds were leaving to return to their homes. I didn't feel as if I had one. I closed my eyes and prayed. "If I'm a daughter of the king, please forgive me. I'm sorry for my wrong attitude."

Nothing changed on the outside, but I felt better on the inside. Four sets of eyes watched me. They needed me to take care of them. Who was I, to think that I could do anything on my own?

"We must go back to the home the king has given me. Maybe my life will be better if I have a different attitude. 'My yoke is easy,' the king said. Let's go."

We arrived as darkness settled. I took the animals to the cave, kissed them good night, and returned to my room. Mari locked me inside and took the key.

"Scylla was sick all day," Mari said. "She never knew you were gone."

"Thanks," I told her.

Mari smiled and waved as she headed down the stairs.

I moaned. Why did the king want me here? Submission? Acceptance of those things I couldn't change?

Several months passed. One night, after a lonely day, I wrote in my diary:

. . .

"Dear Dog, I count it as all joy, the loss of my freedom, believing you have better things for me in the future. Please help me with unbelief that crouches at my heart."

Some nights I cried myself to sleep, but now that Mari trusted me, she would unlock the door when Scylla wasn't home or sleeping. Then I could visit the animals.

As time passed, I grew accustomed to Judd and not as fearful to be around him, although I still refused to talk to him. Was he, indeed, a follower of the king? I struggled to believe it was possible. At times, I still wanted to hate him, for he had not suffered like me. On those days, I prayed hard for the king to help me.

I had forgiven enough to please the king, but not so much that I gave up all my pain. Fear and worry had been my constant companions since birth. Even if I gave them up on a good day, when I was feeling strong, one or the other would return and torture me the next day or the next. I didn't know how to make forgiveness stick. I didn't know how not to worry.

Even if I could, what would fill up that huge hole in my heart the unwanted intruders left behind? I didn't know how to be like the king, even though I tried.

Months passed. Scylla fell into deep depression and rarely came out of her private quarters. Sometimes I'd hear her cry out—although I never understood what she said. She was battling dark demons—enough to keep her locked away for a long time. I was disappointed my father had not returned and that I had not heard from Daniel.

Each day I wrote in my diary another utterance of the king. I prayed his words would become real to me—real enough that I'd be filled with his joy.

"Blessed are the poor in spirit: for theirs is the kingdom of heaven.

Blessed are they that mourn: for they shall be comforted."

. . .

I lamented. If only I could remember the rest that the king said. When would I hear his voice again?

CHAPTER 33

T ERRIBLE NEWS

The king's teachings filled my heart—words of love, joy, peace, patience, and kindness. One afternoon, I was lying on the soft grass in the field and sharing a quiet moment with the animals. Lowly was scratching her back with her legs pumping in the air. Much-Afraid was chasing Cherios. I loved watching them frolic together. A cool breeze pushed the clouds lazily by. The puffy billows reminded me of cotton candy I bought at the fair a long time ago—the time I got sick on the roller coaster.

The chirping of the birds, the buzzing of the insects, even the sounds of silence became gifts that enriched my life. I came to appreciate the value of owning nothing and the lavishness of the ordinary.

Each day, as I enjoyed the beauty of my surroundings, his words came to me and I wrote them down:

. . .

"Consider the lilies how they grow: they toil not, they spin not; and yet I say unto you, that Solomon in all his glory was not arrayed like one of these."

Still, a shadow lingered over me, and sadness ate at my heart.

I heard Worldly Crow before I saw him. Flapping wings announced his arrival. I peered at him upside-down as I was on my back. "I haven't seen you in a while."

"I bring terrible news."

My heart fluttered, and I scooted up to look directly at him. "What news?"

"The king is dead."

"What?" I cried out. "That's impossible."

"The king has been killed—he was hung on a tree between two robbers. Only criminals die like that. Some friends took down his body, and they put him in the borrowed grave of a rich man. It's Passover for the Jews. They couldn't leave a dead body hanging over Passover."

I sat stunned—speechless. How could the king have died? I hunched over, grabbing my stomach. "No, it can't be."

"What are you talking about? Who is dead?" Cherios asked.

Lowly and Much-Afraid came running. "What happened, Shale, what happened to the king?"

"Worldly Crow says the king is dead."

Worldly Crow wiped his eye with his wing, as if he were shedding a tear. He added. "Also, a strange thing happened on the way over here."

Whatever happened couldn't make up for what had already taken place. I covered my face in my hands. Tears fell uncontrollably. "I can't believe anyone would want to kill him."

Cherios scooted up close and laid her head in my lap. "The king can't die," she said. "He's immobile."

"I wish you were right, Cherios," I sobbed, "but I think you mean immortal."

Lowly sat beside me wetting the ground with pig tears. Much-Afraid buried her head between her paws.

"We need to tell Baruch," I heaved.

"I'll go get him," Lowly said. "He's feeding on the oats in the cave."

Worldly Crow cleared his throat and flapped his wings. "A vulture told me on the way over here the king didn't die. He knows where he is."

I stopped crying as Worldly Crow's words sunk into my heart. "What do you mean, he hasn't died? You said he died and was buried in the tomb of a rich man."

"There are many stories circulating in Jerusalem. I don't know what to believe, but the vulture insisted he knows all about the king. He said if you want to see him, for me to bring you."

"A vulture would take me to the king?"

"That's what he told me."

"Vultures eat dead things. Why would I listen to a vulture?"

"*Ca-ca.* Suppose he's right? He seemed informed about these things. The vulture knows more about you than I do."

"Like what?"

"He said you came from far away, that you have friends from the garden, and you should bring your friends, too."

I bit my lip and studied Worldly Crow. Could I trust him?

I covered my face overwhelmed with grief. "What should I do?"

"We must go with you," Cherios said. "The king might need help." She wiggled her nose.

Much-Afraid agreed. "Wherever you go, we shall go with you. We're friends forever, right?"

"Of course." If the king were dead, though, did I even want to live? Suppose the vultures had set a trap? Did vultures eat young girls?

Baruch ran up to me, nostrils flared and breathing heavily. His eyes bulged, disturbed by the news from Worldly Crow. "Is it true, Miss Shale? No one would kill the king, would they?"

"Not unless he let them." I remembered the day when the underling offered the king everything, and he turned it all down. The angels came and brought him food.

I returned to the present. Why would anyone do such a thing? I jumped up and hugged Baruch. "Oh, Baruch, what shall we do? You're wise. Tell me what to do. Worldly Crow says a vulture wants to take us to the king—all of us."

Tears coated Baruch's extra-long eyelashes. "Then we must go. Friends never abandon friends in their need. He's more than a friend. He's our king. Yes, we must go. We must go right away."

I glanced up at Worldly Crow. "Are you sure, Worldly Crow? The vulture doesn't want to eat us, does he?"

"Vultures don't kill things to eat. They eat what is already dead."

I became teary-eyed as I recalled the king—all the magnificent words he uttered and the way he looked at me. I couldn't bear to think he might be dead. "We shall go and see about the king. After all, he would do the same for us. We'll go, all of us."

I looked across the land at my father's flocks and estate. "I must say good-bye to Mari, in case we don't come back."

"Suppose she tries to stop you?" Much-Afraid asked.

"I have a feeling I may not see her again, and she's been my friend for the last year, since Daniel and my father left." I glanced around. "Does anyone know where Judd is?"

"In the cave," Lowly said.

"I wonder if he knows." I risked a lot—possibly locked up for good. "I can't go back," I whispered, "to say good-bye."

"Why do you talk as if you aren't coming back?" Baruch asked.

"Suppose it's a trap?"

Worldly Crow impatiently strutted back and forth on the branch. "Are we going or not?"

"Yes. Let's go." I picked up Cherios and climbed on Baruch's back.

Lowly looked forlorn, hanging his head. "I don't think I can go. It would look strange to have a pig walking alongside the road outside of Gadara. Jews don't like pigs. I shouldn't tempt fate."

I hopped off Baruch and approached Lowly. It wasn't enough to pat him on the head. I gave him a big hug. "I love you, Lowly." I remembered the first time he saw the king and how afraid he was of being eaten. Thank goodness, he didn't drown in the lake. "You mind the stable, okay?"

A tear dropped from Lowly's eye. "I'll look for you every minute until your return. You will return, won't you?"

"I hope so, Lowly. If I don't, you've seen the king. You know the king's love. You won't forget, will you?"

Lowly shook his head.

I climbed on Baruch's back. "Let's go, Worldly Crow."

CHAPTER 34

B ETRAYAL

The journey was long. A journey always seems longer or harder when one fears death is the destination. Several hours passed, night fell, and the shadows followed me, even more than when the underlings banished us from the garden. This darkness seeped into the land of the living from the underworld—where wolves howled, owls hooted, and trees creaked. Earthquakes beneath the ground ruptured the foundations of the living, but if the worst event in history had already happened, the world couldn't get any grimmer.

Nothing could fill the void within me. The stars appeared as if they might fall from the heavens. Dark, shadowy figures emerged from behind rocks, trees, and holes in the ground. Soon a vulture flew overhead leading Worldly Crow and the rest of us to a place I didn't want to go.

"When will we arrive, Worldly Crow?" I asked.

"Not too much farther. We're close to the city."

Where was the king? I remembered the king's words, his miracles, and his promises. I filled my mind with the stories he told on the mountaintop, although I anticipated a terrible ending for us all.

Did the world kill the king or did the king die because he chose it? I was willing to die for my king, but fear seized my heart as I cradled Cherios in my arms.

Much-Afraid trotted beside us speaking soothing words. "We're with you Shale. Don't be afraid."

A male voice spoke to me. I did not know who she was. She spoke about things I wasn't sure I understood—haunting words. "The worst of the underlings deceived those who weren't teachable as little children. The vile creatures will continue to deceive those who refuse to believe. The universe mourns. The tears shed in the garden haven't dried."

The voice continued. "The greatest miracle will soon be revealed. Face the secret hidden in your heart. Confess so you may be healed. You've been brought to a place of decision. Redemption is a gift only the king can give."

I became very quiet as the male voice continued. "Remember all you've heard. Do not be deceived. Quote the words of the king as you remember them. He'll tell you what to say. Tonight, all the inhabitants in the garden mourn. The eternal light has become sin, but only for a brief time. The underlings want to devour all who refuse to believe in the truth. Don't compromise." Then the voice ceased.

"You look like you saw a ghost," Much-Afraid said.

"No, no ghost. A voice spoke to me from the king's kingdom."

I brooded whenever I started to doubt. Waves of despair washed over me. The Hall of Darkness wanted to hold me captive. I was determined to resist.

"Come quickly," Worldly Crow urged. "Hurry." He blended into a ghastly-looking tree.

"Are you sure this isn't a trap?"

"I'm taking you to the king. That is what you want, right?"

"Yes."

"The vulture said they have the king."

Graves opened and underlings rode the four winds that rustled through the trees. In the high places and the low places, the vultures squeaked and squawked. The shadows deepened, and all light departed from the living.

A dozen vultures flew towards us and landed in a palm dressed up like a scarecrow. My hands were cold, barely warmed by Cherios's body. My heart pounded, and I labored to breathe.

Underlings ran out of the cave and hissed. Two of the bat creatures grabbed me on each side, forcing me off Baruch and squeezing my arms.

"Let go. You're hurting me," I cried.

Their constant laughter and taunting drowned out my pleas.

They took us inside a damp, dark cave where the vile creatures ripped me from my friends. I didn't know where the others were taken. The sinewy birds tied me to a martyr's stone and bound my hands and feet with a thick, scratchy rope. I couldn't move. In a distant chamber, sharp cries pieced the silence.

"Tis the night," one vulture shouted, and others chimed in. Their chants increased, and they flew about me in an irregular circular pattern. Their mockery of my capture seemed like perverted foolishness.

I shut my eyes to avoid seeing the terrifying display, but their screams were harder to ignore. I cried out, but fear muffled my words. Every time a wing flapped near me, I cringed. The cold draft sent chills down my arms and legs.

I squirmed within the bindings, but they dug deeper into my skin. Something touched me from behind. More shape shifters appeared, like bats without a body, spiritual beings somewhere between a gas and a liquid. My cold hands lost all feeling. I gulped in the damp air.

The underlings laughed and hissed. Shadows swung back and forth imitating the cartoon characters on my bedroom walls. A creature smacked me repeatedly from behind.

The shape shifter laughed. "Look."

"I can't. The bindings are too tight."

"Bring the prisoners before her," he demanded.

A demon stepped forward and thrust a terrified creature in front of me. The battered animal landed at my feet.

"Cherios," I cried.

Her sad eyes ripped at my heart.

"Make her talk," the underling demanded. "Come on, show us. Animals can't talk."

"Yes, they can," I said.

"You're powerless here," the underling hissed. The taunting continued. Cherios stared at the dirt floor.

"Bring the next one."

The shape shifters released Much-Afraid, and she squirmed across the floor to me. Her warm tongue on my toes tingled like a healing balm from the king.

The dark powers regrouped. "The dumb animals can't talk anymore," a demon shouted. Others chimed. "Death to Shale, death to the animals, and death to their king."

"Tell them your secret," another one demanded. "You're bad, Shale Snyder."

The circle of demons expanded. Even in the darkness, I could still see a little. The underlings grew bigger and more powerful as they fed on my fear. I prayed for light.

Baruch heehawed.

"Kick him," one of the demons demanded.

"I'll never kick Baruch," I fired back.

"Kick him. We know what you do to animals," another one hissed.

Baruch's eyes bulged. He whinnied and ducked his head. Much-Afraid cowered, pawing at the dirt. Was Cherios still alive?

If only the king could rescue us, if only he were here. The vultures tricked Worldly Crow. Where were all those followers who sat on the hills and listened to the king?

Jeers went up from the demons. They shouted, "The battle is over, we have won, the tables are turned, redemption spurned."

CHAPTER 35

T HE BATTLE

Invisible drums beat an Indian battle cry. The leader of the demons slithered in, and his bat wings spanned the walls of the cave. He held in his claws *The Book of Remembrance*. "Our latest trophy."

The underlings gathered around the flat stone where I sat bound in ropes. Round and round they circled, chanting curses and snorting a potion. The nefarious spirits soured my stomach, and their evilness rattled my nerves. I wouldn't give in, though. I was a daughter of the king.

Hate stabbed at my soul, and the weight of evil wanted to overwhelm me. I resisted. I remembered the weight of glory. The underlings chanted louder. They desired my soul. I remembered what the king said.

"Do not fear, for you are more valuable than many sparrows."

I fell through a dark hole into a bottomless pit. I quoted the words of the king again. "Do not fear those which kill the body, but can't kill the soul. Rather, fear him which is able to destroy both soul and body in hell."

Their chants drowned out my words. I must not let anger or fear control me. The demons were the Olympians of hate.

Their noxious breath made me nauseous. I turned away. I tried to loosen my hands, but the ropes burned my wrists. Cruel images tormented my mind.

"Hate," they chanted.

I cried out to the king. "Deliver me from evil, for you are the kingdom, the power, and the glory, forever and ever."

Their chants continued.

The demons' dark magic revealed a hallway full of kids. A boy with a Braves cap covering his eyes came up from behind me. He snuck in front of a student. I felt his fingers where they shouldn't be. I turned around to face him. Judd laughed. I hated him—no. Anger welled up inside of me—no. I became depressed every time I hated him. Deep within my heart, I remembered the words of the king and his love for me. I remembered his command and recited the words by heart. "You shall love the Lord your God with all your heart and with all your soul and with all your might."

The king's words grew inside of me, words gushing forth from my heart as I needed them. Then I realized, the demons didn't want to kill me. They wanted to possess me—like the cemetery man. They needed a body.

Much-Afraid cried out. "I love you."

Cherios hopped up on a stone slab and gazed at me with her trusting brown eyes. "I love you, too," she said. "Keep saying the words of the king."

For a tiny moment, the demons seemed disoriented. A flash of light skimmed across the cave ceiling.

"So the little rabbit loves you, huh?" an underling mocked.

The bat creatures gathered around displaying needle stingers that protruded from their midsection. They wanted to zap me on my legs or arms. I tried to avoid the stingers, but one still stung my leg. I felt a twinge of pain, but the sensation disappeared—miraculously. Then I couldn't catch my breath. It was as if I had fallen into a cold spring and had the wind knocked out of me.

The underlings chanted again. "Death to the animals, death to Shale, she belongs in hell."

Ice tentacles crept up from my hands into my shoulders. I shivered. How much longer could I take this torment?

Much-Afraid cried out. "Don't give in. Hold on. Don't believe their lies. Remember the words of the king."

Baruch whinnied and tried to bolt, but his tether prevented him from leaving. A demon flashed a sword at him. He whinnied, but when the sword landed on him, it bounced off, not even piercing his skin.

"Forget the donkey. He's not who we want," a demon shrieked.

The underlings gathered around me. They untied the rope, but two still held me on each side. The demons took me to a darkened archway. The hallway was long and became narrower as we neared the end. On the other side, a door opened to mysterious stairs, but once I stood at the top, I knew where I was.

The demon in charge demanded. "Bring the animals to the front."

Baruch, Cherios, and Much-Afraid stood beside me. Their eyes questioned me.

"Tell them what you see, Shale. What is at the bottom of the stairs?"

I refused to look.

"Look," the demon demanded.

"No."

"Look now or you can watch your friends die a slow death."

Momentary fear swept across their faces.

"Please don't harm them."

The demon holding Cherios quipped. "We're waiting."

A theatrical scene began. I stood at the top of the stairs with Fifi under my arm. I held my mother's iPhone in my hand. As I stepped down the stairs, I texted a message. Fifi squirmed. I tried to catch him before he slipped, but he knocked the iPhone out of my hand. I reached out to catch it—more afraid I'd break the iPhone than hurt the dog. I had taken the iPhone from Mother without asking.

I missed the step and fell, dropping the dog. The iPhone bounced on the steps. I fell on top of Fifi. He yelped and flopped down a couple more. I fell forward and knocked him again. He rolled the rest of the way. My ankle twisted underneath me, and I couldn't move, except to fall head-first. I braced myself to avoid hitting my face. At the bottom of the stairs, Fifi lay motionless.

He opened his mouth gasping for breath—air that never came. His eyes were still open. I picked up his still, warm body and cradled him. Tears streamed from my eyes.

What had I done? I killed Judd's puppy—all to keep from breaking my mother's iPhone. How could I tell anyone it was an accident when I had been so foolish?

I tore my eyes away from the horrific scene to face my friends—Baruch, Much-Afraid, and Cherios.

"I didn't mean to. It was an accident."

"It's Fifi," Cherios said.

How did Cherios know his name? The few seconds that passed seemed like forever. Why did the demons reveal my shame? It was enough I did it and was unable to forgive myself.

The demons set Cherios down, untied Baruch, and released Much-Afraid.

The underlings continued to accuse me. "She deceived all of you."

I shouted back. "I made a mistake. That doesn't make me bad."

The underlings became silent. Then the chants began again. The more hate-filled their words, the bigger they became.

The king's power filled my mind. Goose bumps tingled from my heart and spread. A warm light pierced the cold darkness, and the oppression lifted.

"Yes, you're right. I am nothing more than a worm, like that worm lying on the sidewalk that Judd wanted to crush. Nothing good inside me exists except that given me by the king. Just as I rescued that worm from his tormenter, my king will rescue me, too, and crush your head. The king promised. "If you forgive others, your heavenly father will also forgive you. I am forgiven."

Cherios smiled from ear to ear. "Yes, Shale. You know the king."

Much-Afraid nodded.

Baruch's eyes glistened—no longer with mournful tears but grateful praise.

Magical stirrings from deep within bubbled forth and overflowed. Freedom beckoned me.

The biggest demon jeered, "The king is dead."

Others chanted and danced. "The king is dead, the king is dead, the underlings will rule instead."

I countered their lies, "He'll always live in my heart. You can't hurt me anymore." I quoted the king again. "There is no fear in love. Perfect love casts out fear."

My shouts of praise to the king overcame their chants. Suddenly, the demons began to shrink—smaller and smaller, right before my eyes. As the underlings shrunk, they underwent a metamorphosis.

I shouted to my animal friends. "Join me in praises to the king."

We sang our own song and drowned out theirs. "Blessed be the king forever and ever."

They shrank smaller and smaller, and we grew larger and larger. Soon the underlings had shape shifted into nothing more than puny snakes. Even though they hissed, their voices became as a little mouse's before a taunting cat.

I raised my hands in praise to the king. "To whom is the glory for ever and ever. I know who I am. I am a princess—a daughter of the king."

Joy flowed through my veins. We had conquered hate with love! Then something tragic happened.

CHAPTER 36

SECRETS OF THE GARDEN

Cherios was hopping on the ledge celebrating when a snake lashed out and struck her. She screamed and fell, landing at my feet. I scooped her in my arms, much as I had held Fifi after he died. Cherios's eyes seemed far away, and her labored breathing scared me.

"Don't die, Cherios, you mustn't. I love you too much."

As the tiny vipers raced off in the darkness, Much-Afraid and Baruch ran up to me. My heart was broken.

"What should we do?" I cried.

"Is she still alive?" Baruch asked.

"Barely." I sniffled. "Cherios, can you hear me?"

Cherios forced her eyes open one last time. "I'd die for you anytime because I love you so much."

"No, Cherios, you mustn't die. No."

Cherios whispered. "Take me to the garden, to the apple tree."

"What do you mean the garden and the apple tree?"

"To the garden when we arrived," Baruch said. "She's a garden bunny. She wants to go home."

The vipers were gone. Nothing held us back from escaping. The demons fled when we defeated them with the king's love. Suddenly, faraway sounds echoed through the narrow passages—what might it be but another demon?

I held Cherios in my arms afraid even to breathe. A strong body walked out of the dark hole behind us. I was too shocked to speak.

Daniel's eyes met mine. "Shale, what are you doing here?"

"How did you find me?"

"I could read your mind—terrifying images. I told you before, the next time I wouldn't delay. I hurried here as fast as I could." Daniel surveyed the dark cave. "Are you okay?"

"I think so, but Cherios isn't. We must get her back to the garden, but I don't know the way."

"I know," Baruch said. "We need to go to the olive garden in Jerusalem."

"We need to go to the olive garden in Jerusalem," I repeated for Daniel. "That's where Cherios asked to be buried, at the apple tree."

Daniel stared at me. "You mean the Garden of Gethsemane? You don't want to go there. Violence erupted the other night. Soldiers captured your king while he was praying and took him to Pontius Pilate. After beating the man, the Roman guards sent him to the high priest. The council put him on trial and found him guilty of blasphemy. He was crucified."

I shook my head in disbelief.

"The place is crawling with guards. There are stories about him returning from the dead. The last place you want to go is to that garden. You should bury her here instead."

"So he was killed?"

"They placed a sign over his crucifixion, 'King of the Jews.'"

I sobbed, laying my head on Daniel's chest.

He placed his hand on my shoulder. "I'm sorry, Shale."

I lowered my eyes and wrapped Cherios in my arms. Her body was still warm. What else could go wrong? I didn't want to risk being caught. Daniel draped his arm around me and directed me back to the entrance.

"Daniel, we have to take her to the olive garden."

"If that is what you must do, we better hurry and do it before daylight." Daniel shook his head. "I can't believe you want to go there."

"I'm sorry."

"It's okay. Let's go."

Daniel patted me reassuringly.

I couldn't talk. My voice was stuck deep down in my throat.

We left the cave in surreal darkness. Everywhere were underlings —on top of the mountains, hiding behind trees, and rising from the crevasses. Their rancid smell turned my stomach. I imagined graves opening and demons escaping that would torture me again.

Before we reached the garden, I panicked. "Daniel, there weren't any apple trees in the garden. There were olive trees and thorns and a wolf."

"Why would Cherios tell you to take her to the apple tree in the garden if there wasn't an apple tree there?" Daniel asked.

"I don't know."

"She dumped the apple core on the ground when she popped out of the knapsack," Baruch said. "Remember, she apologized for eating my apple."

"That was how long ago?" I asked.

"What?" Daniel couldn't understand the donkey.

"Baruch said she ate his apple. It's been, what, three years? Maybe an apple tree grew from the seed. It's been long enough."

We traveled over the rough terrain, not saying anything else. The full moon rose overhead and began its descent as we passed through the Kidron Valley.

When we arrived, a guard was on duty, and the garden was closed. Since when did gardens need a guard?

Daniel whispered, "I'll distract the guard so you can sneak past. I'll follow you later. Okay?"

I nodded. Daniel approached the man, and once the guard's back was turned, I snuck all of us in—Baruch, Much-Afraid, Cherios, and myself. Now we would have to search for the tree. Cherios's lifeless body was getting colder. I worried we were too late to save her. If so, I wanted to bury her as soon as possible.

"Look over there." Baruch pointed to a tree—one lone apple tree in a thicket of olive trees.

The apple tree stood about seven feet tall. "I can't believe it, Baruch." Bright red apples covered the branches and appeared delicious even in the dim light from the moon. Something about it seemed odd—the tree didn't belong. How would Cherios have known the tree was here?

I swung down off Baruch as Much-Afraid dug into the ground with her paws to loosen the dirt. Baruch joined in helping Much-Afraid, and I stood by and watched. Everything seemed so final. I wanted to return her to the king's garden where she belonged, but this would have to do —it was what she asked.

Soon the hole was deep enough to bury her. I laid her gently in the cool sand. The strong scent from the apple tree bathed the air as a healing balm. I remembered the day in the king's garden when I first arrived. A garden peace replaced my anxiety. Cherios would rest here, maybe not in the king's garden, but under the king's apple tree.

Baruch started to cover up Cherios with the dirt, but I asked him to wait. I felt the egg in my dress pocket. I'd give it to her.

I pulled the egg out of my pocket and opened it. After lifting out one of the rabbits, I held it up in the moonlight. Belief and disbelief hit me at once. No longer was the bunny broken. I put the bunny back in the egg and lifted up the mother. She was a perfectly carved rabbit, as were all the others.

"What's the matter with the egg and bunnies?" Baruch asked.

"They—they aren't broken anymore."

"Look," Much-Afraid said.

I glanced down at Cherios and thought she moved. I put my hand in front of her mouth and felt her soft breath. "She—she's breathing," I stammered.

"She can't be breathing. She's dead." The voice was familiar but it wasn't Much-Afraid or Baruch.

I glanced up and saw Worldly Crow sitting on a branch of the apple tree. "Get out of here."

The crow talked in a cheeky voice. "Now look. Don't be angry with me."

"You nearly got us killed. Of course I'm angry with you."

"*Ca-ca.* I took you to the king, didn't I?"

"No, you did not. You took us to demons and shape shifters who tried to kill us. They almost killed Cherios."

"The vultures said they captured the king."

"Go away," I demanded. "Leave us alone."

"I'll be back," Worldly Crow insisted, "with those who hold your king captive. He's not what he seems—he's no king at all. He lied to the people. You can trust me. Better one fool dies than all the people."

With that, the crow took off. Good riddance. I wanted nothing to do with him.

Much-Afraid scooted up to Cherios and licked her face. "She's coming around, Shale."

Baruch leaned down and sniffed—as he had done long ago when I slapped him for getting too close to me. Cherios's whiskers tickled him, and he heehawed.

"Are you sure?" I crouched down to see for myself. Cherios flickered her eyes and opened them.

"Cherios—you're alive. How could you come back to life?"

"I'm a bunny from the king's garden," she said. "He's the gardener."

"But Worldly Crow said the king is dead. How can he heal others and not heal himself?" I asked.

"Wait until the morning, and you shall know. For now, let me sleep." Cherios closed her eyes with a broad smile on her face. Could the king still be alive? What did Worldly Crow know? The demons seemed impotent. After all, did I not defeat them with the king's love?

I looked around for Daniel. I wished he would show up. "Come," I said. "Let's huddle up together and keep warm."

LORILYN ROBERTS

The night air was cool. I didn't want to leave the healing apple tree and hoped by morning Daniel would find us. We would wait. I blew on my hands and snuggled up to Much-Afraid and Cherios.

But Baruch wouldn't lie down.

"What's wrong, Baruch? Come on, we need you to keep us warm."

"First I want an apple," Baruch said.

"An apple?"

"Maybe two or three. I'm hungry."

I shook my head at my favorite donkey.

CHAPTER 37

MYSTERIES OF THE SEVENTH DIMENSION

Disturbing dreams of jeering crowds and angry mobs on the streets of Jerusalem made it difficult to sleep. A Roman guard with a cat o'nine tail thrashed the king, who wore a crown of thorns. Stripes of blood covered his back. Nails hammered into his wrists and ankles left marks of unimaginable pain. I twisted and turned as the terrifying images awoke me.

Suddenly a violent shaking of the ground ended any thought of sleep. Running feet and men's voices disturbed the silence. I sat up but couldn't see anything. A little later, distraught voices of women filled the garden. Groggy, I wanted to find them. I got up, leaving Cherios, Much-Afraid and Baruch, and crept over to an olive tree. Oil had beaded up on the leaves and was dripping down the sides of the trunk. The tree was weeping.

I snatched off a leaf, dipped my finger into the oil, and rubbed the oil into my hands. I rubbed more oil on my arms and face. My dirtiness and sorrow eased, as if the oil had healing properties.

I stood and watched two women huddled around an opening to a cave. Next to the opening was a large stone. The women's eyes were red and swollen. They carried burial herbs.

Two creatures in brightly-lit garments appeared beside them. I nearly fainted at their appearance. The frightened women bowed with their faces to the ground.

One of the angels said, "He is not here, but he has risen. Remember how he spoke to you while he was still in Galilee."

The women appeared confused, but remained quiet.

I stared, recalling the words of the king—and the angel spoke to the women similarly—"The Son of Man must be delivered into the hands of sinful men, and be crucified, and the third day rise again."

A loud commotion took place outside the garden a few furlongs away. I was surprised to see Worldly Crow arguing with three underlings. The entrance to the garden was blocked by a man dressed in a white robe. The king's power had usurped the evil presence that lurked outside the garden. I sensed the magnificent parting of evil—magnificent because never again would evil be able to triumph. The underlings and Worldly Crow fled, screeching in torment and submissive in defeat —their fate sealed.

Then the king stood before the women. I gasped. "He's alive!" I said, under my breath. My heart burned within me as I thought about the enormity of what it meant—and remembered what he said on the mountain. The women appeared not to recognize him. Perhaps they thought he was the gardener.

The king said to one of them, "Woman, why are you weeping? Whom are you seeking?"

She replied, "Sir, if you have carried him away, tell me where you have laid him, and I will take him away."

The king said, "Mary."

The woman turned towards him and cried out. "Teacher!"

The king replied. "Stop clinging to me, for I have not yet ascended to the Father; but go to my brethren and say to them, 'I ascend to my father and your father, and my God and your God.'"

The women took off, running.

The king turned towards me. I now knew the king completely—as my heavenly father, the father who loved me, the father who would never leave me or forsake me.

He held out his hands and the fresh scars on his wrists over-whelmed me. "Your sins are forgiven."

My tears flowed freely.

He said, "I go to prepare a place for you. If I go and prepare a place for you, I will come again and receive you to myself, that where I am, there you may be also."

A birdcage gently floated down from the sky and landed in his outstretched hand. He took the cage and hung it on an olive tree. A small bird sat inside the cage. The king opened the door to the cage, and the small creature walked from its perch and alighted on his finger. He lifted the bird out of the cage, kissed it, and whispered, "You are a daughter of the king."

I realized, at that moment he was saying those words to me. I felt his tender kiss on my forehead.

I gazed into the sky as the bird flew into the heavens. Before I could say anything, the king was gone.

A male voice called my name. "Shale."

I felt an otherworldly garden presence before I saw him. He was beautiful to behold, dressed in dazzling white.

"I recognize your voice, but who are you? I know the king, but I don't know you."

"I'm your guardian angel, Astello."

The angel wore a shimmering white robe. "Do not be afraid."

"You spoke all those words to me. Why are you here?"

"I have come to take you home. Your journey to the seventh dimension is finished—for the moment."

"The seventh dimension? Is that where I've been? I thought I went back in time."

"The seventh dimension is where the king lives—in the garden, in the great city, in the wilderness, in the secret place of your heart. Reality is transcended in this world that even the angels find hard to understand."

"Does everyone go back in time?"

"No. The king meets people where they are. A person can even turn away from the king—but the king knows his own, and he'll pursue the lost soul until the person can no longer hear his voice at all."

"How tragic," I whispered.

"People journey to the seventh dimension when something happens that creates a longing—so great that nothing else can fill it, except the king himself."

"That's how it was for me. I knew I wanted something, but I didn't know what it was. The longing wouldn't go away."

Astello smiled. "Those who read the Bible go back in time and meet the king. The king opens the door to all who knock. The road is narrow. Many are called, few are chosen."

"Daniel said it was a parallel universe."

"Science can't unravel the mysteries of the spiritual realm. They are too deep, but Daniel is searching, and the king will find him."

"Must I leave?" I did not want to go. "What about Baruch, Much-Afraid, Cherios, and Daniel?"

"They will be safe in the king's love. What did the king tell you?"

"I am a daughter of the king."

Astello nodded. "You're like Neveah. Free to live your life for the king—or not. The choice is yours."

"I realize now, as a daughter of the king, I'm never alone."

Three of my favorite animals came over to me.

"An angel!" Cherios beamed.

"You woke up and are alive!" I picked up Cherios and kissed her. "You see Astello?"

Cherios's eyes shone brightly with her life restored. "Of course I see him."

"We all see him because we believe," added Much-Afraid.

Tears filled my eyes. "It's time for me to go home. I hate to leave you."

We spent several minutes hugging each other and remembering all the times we shared in the seventh dimension. I shed more tears over our imminent separation than I had ever shed in the past.

The angel said, "Treasure all these things in your heart. Take the egg with you as a remembrance."

"What about my friends here?"

Astello replied, "Daniel can't leave the seventh dimension yet. Perhaps you will meet again."

"Can I say good-bye to him?"

"He'll be here soon. The king planned it this way from the beginning."

"What about Baruch?"

"He knows the king."

"*Heehaw.* I used to hate carrying things on my back. I'm no longer a beast of burden. I have carried a daughter of the king."

Astello explained. "Baruch was burdened by many things not meant for him to carry—things only the king could carry."

"And Lowly?" I asked.

"He has adventures yet ahead in the seventh dimension."

"And I promise you, Shale," Baruch said, "I'll tell Lowly everything so he'll know you made it home safely."

My eyes watered and I blinked to hold back tears. "He's such a sweet pig. I'll miss him."

Cherios begged. "Hold me one last time."

I patted her on the head and ran my fingers through her soft fur. I didn't want to believe this would be the last time I would hold her.

Astello paused. "Gifts come in many forms—but the seventh dimension is the best."

"I don't understand."

"When you arrive home, you will see."

Cherios squirmed out of my arms. "Do I get to go home now?" she asked.

Astello nodded.

Cherios bounced up and down. Then, seeing how sad I was, she hopped back into my arms. "Oh, Shale, don't be sad. I will always be with you. You will see."

How could I be so joyful and sad at the same time? "What about Much-Afraid?"

The dog stood with her eyes to the ground and her tail between her legs.

The angel smiled. "Much-Afraid, why are you and Shale so sad? Whatever is bound in the seventh dimension is bound on earth."

"Much-Afraid does come with me?" I asked.

"Of course Much-Afraid comes with you."

I squatted down and clasped my arms around her. With much exuberance, she knocked me backwards and licked me on the forehead.

Astello reminded me. "Remember all the king has done. Some you won't understand until later. The hard things will make you strong if you let them. Bitterness will creep in if you allow a foothold. It only takes a foothold to become a stronghold."

I treasured in my heart all the counsel Astello gave me. "Could you explain once more about the seventh dimension? I want to be able to tell Rachel where I've been."

"The seventh dimension is within you. When you call out to the king, he takes you to a place where he can perform magic not found in this world—a magic that goes back before the curse and deeper than evil can reach. Even angels long to understand this mystery."

I reflected on the past three years. Troubled, I asked. "Will I see my father again?"

"Do you want to?"

"I don't know. If he loved me, surely he would have sent letters to me from Jerusalem, or taken responsibility for his absence. I don't want anything to do with his wife."

"It requires humility to face our mistakes. Don't give up hope."

"Things will never be perfect here, will they?"

"If it were possible, the king would not have been crucified. He died for all—those who love the king will one day live in the king's garden with him."

"He's alive!"

"He is risen indeed."

"Why was he slain?"

The angel explained. "In the beginning, the king created a beautiful garden. He made all the plants and animals. Then he created Adam and Eve. He declared that everything was good."

"One day the serpent convinced Eve to eat a fruit from a tree the king told her not to eat from. After she ate of it, she gave the fruit from the same tree to Adam."

"Their eyes were opened. Fear, one of the first symptoms of sin, entered the garden. The king knew there was only one way to get rid of this terrible disease. He had to be slain."

"When the king died on the cross, he broke the dark magic of the underlings—the power of the serpent. The king's death made it possible for everyone to live in the garden of heaven."

"I saw the scars on his hands."

"Anyone who asks for forgiveness and believes in the king will live forever in the king's garden."

"Will the king always be with me?"

"Always. The seventh dimension is within you. The animals represent parts of your character. Your suffering has produced good fruit. And always remember, the king is your heavenly father."

"What about Judd?"

"Forgiving him set you free. No one is beyond the king's power. You must forgive everyone, just as the king has forgiven you—even forgiving yourself sometimes."

Astello cautioned. "Don't let a day go by without giving thanks, even for the hard things."

"Will Nathan be all right?"

"Nathan and all those who come to the king. The king is the great healer."

Astello continued. "While you may be impatient and want things right away, it is in the process that you glorify the king. The outcome is in his scarred hands."

He smiled. "Look behind you. Daniel is coming."

I turned as he approached.

His eyes met mine. "Sorry I didn't come last night. I was detained."

We embraced for a minute and I felt his heart beating. "I must go, Daniel. It's time."

"Then I guess I came to say good-bye."

A sadness in his voice made me weep.

I clutched him tighter. "I wish I'd asked the angel more about you. I was saving you for last, but I ran out of time. Too many questions filled my mind. My father, how is he?"

Daniel stroked my hair. "He's fine. I wish he had made an effort to see you—as I have."

"Oh, Daniel, I hate to leave. The angel said we would meet again —possibly."

"The angel?"

"Daniel, you must believe in the king. He is who he says he is. Your life depends on it. He's risen."

Daniel laughed. "Risen? Calm down. I'll be helping Doctor Luke. He wants to do an investigation into his claims. I know there's something different about this man. I want to know the truth."

"Will you be at my father's estate or with the doctor?"

Daniel lifted up my face to his. "Both. I don't understand the mystery in all of this, but I will. Tell Rachel shalom for me when you return home."

"I will."

Daniel continued. "That you met me is strange enough. I want to learn more about this man of God."

"Okay," I whispered. "I'll find you in Israel."

Daniel grinned. "I have no doubt that you will."

"I'm already seventeen now. I've been here three years."

"Remember, I'm from your future."

"So you need to be back by 2015 to meet me. You will be back?"

"Do I control that?" Daniel asked.

"Yes. Believe."

"Believe? I need help with my unbelief."

"Daniel, he is risen. The evidence is all around you. Look at Cherios. Where is she, anyway?"

"I'm back here with Baruch and Much-Afraid."

"She's alive!" Daniel asked, "How can she be alive?"

"It is easier to believe in things we can see than to have faith in the power that is unseen, but the things we see are an outward manifestation of that power. Believe me when I tell you."

Daniel patted me on the shoulder. "I will."

I stood back and caught a tear in his eye. "You will take care of Baruch and Lowly?"

"Of course. Aren't you excited you get to go home?"

"Without you, though."

Daniel studied my face. "You're more beautiful the older you get."

I laughed. Maybe the oil had magical qualities.

Daniel's eyes twinkled. "I sense you have something to give me."

"Yes, you reminded me." I reached into my dress pocket and pulled out the two golden nuggets I'd forgotten about.

I handed one to Daniel. "These rocks have burned almost everyone else, but I don't think you'll be hurt."

He turned the stone over in his hand. "Is it gold?"

"Just keep the nugget. It matches mine and is my promise I'll find you in the future. The angel told me I would."

"The angel?" Daniel repeated. "You keep talking about an angel."

I pointed to him. "He's over there. You don't see him?"

Daniel shook his head. "I believe you, though."

"You must believe, Daniel. Your unbelief is holding you back."

"I'm trying, Shale."

"Oh, Daniel, I just remembered something important. Promise me you will go into my private room and retrieve my scrolls. I left them behind and I don't want Scylla to find them."

"Your writings?"

"My diary. Keep it for me until I see you again."

Daniel chuckled. "Can I read it?"

"I suppose, if you can't resist. Don't let anyone else, though. Promise you will get them?"

"I promise."

I picked up Cherios, who was cleaning her paws. "How will you get back?"

"Just as you will, through the door."

"The portal will close soon," Astello said. "The time has come."

I gave Cherios one last hug and set her down. She hopped over and kissed Baruch and Much-Afraid. Then she gave me a wink and hopped through the portal. I watched as two other bunnies greeted her in the king's garden. Soon a dog ran up and joined the rabbits.

"Fifi!" I exclaimed. "Cherios never told me she knew Fifi."

"You never asked." Astello replied.

"I couldn't forgive myself so I never told anyone my secret."

"She knew."

I watched as they hugged and kissed each other. Then the image faded, leaving me sad but also happy.

I glanced down at Much-Afraid. She looked freshly groomed, washed, and combed to perfection. "How did you get so clean? You look as if you made a quick trip to the groomer."

Much-Afraid looked knowingly at Baruch. She pranced around in a circle, showing off her shimmering white coat. "Baruch gave me a good licking and cleaned me up."

I chuckled. "Baruch—you're such a sweet donkey."

"I'd have licked you, too, but I didn't think you'd like that, seeing I'm an ole smelly donkey."

I smiled. "Baruch, you're too much. You'll always be my favorite donkey."

"And you are my favorite young lady, Miss Shale."

I threw Baruch a kiss. We needed to leave before I started crying.

"Are you ready, Much-Afraid?" I asked.

"Whenever you are."

My eyes turned to Daniel. "You promise to wait for me, right? And get my diary?"

He nodded. "Three years."

"Good-bye, Baruch."

"Until we meet again, Miss Shale."

The angel said reassuringly, "The police are looking for you. Everything will be as it was, except the seventh dimension is now within you. Use your gifts wisely. If you do, the king will increase them. If you don't, your gifts will be given to another, although they will never be taken away completely. Hope exists even when you go astray."

I promised, "I will."

CHAPTER 38

E BENEZER

A light shining in my face awakened me.

"Shale, are you okay?" a voice asked.

Another voice shouted. "Come quick, she's over here."

Much-Afraid whimpered as she rested her paws on my stomach. I squinted and covered my eyes with my hand.

"That a girl. You kept her warm, didn't you?" the voice said.

I opened my eyes, focusing on the face overhead. He looked like a police officer. Much-Afraid climbed on my chest and licked me in the face. I chuckled and petted her head.

"That dog saved your life, kiddo. Otherwise, you would have died of exposure last night. It was cold."

"Really?"

"Do you remember tripping over this rock and hitting your head?"

"No, but I want to keep it."

"The dog, you mean?"

"The rock—and the dog."

"The rock you tripped over?" He shook his head. "Why would you want that?"

Much-Afraid and the memory of the rock returned, flooding me with disjointed scenes from the seventh dimension. Soon two more officers ran over and crouched beside me. One pulled out a phone. The other checked my pulse.

"How do you feel?"

I smiled weakly. "My head hurts but other than that, I'm okay."

Two paramedics approached with a stretcher. I insisted that Much-Afraid come with me. "And I want the rock I tripped over."

"Sure thing," the police officer replied.

The medics carried me out to the street where an ambulance was waiting. Mother came running and hovered over me. "Shale, thank God, you're okay."

"I fell and hit my head."

"We didn't know where you were. What were you doing in the woods?"

"I followed Much-Afraid."

"Are you ready?" the officer asked.

"Will you take care of my dog?"

The officer nodded. "Yes, ma'am. No problem."

A short while later, Remi met Mother and me at the emergency room. Finding nothing more than a bump on my head, the doctor gave us the good news. "She's fine. Fix her some homemade chicken soup and give her a couple of days of rest."

When we arrived home, Rachel was waiting for me on the porch. Much-Afraid sat beside her with food and water nearby. A large bone she had nibbled on protruded from the bowl. The woman with Rachel reminded me of Mari.

Much-Afraid yelped. I ran up and knelt beside her, tears in my eyes. She whimpered and pranced around me.

"Thank you, Rachel."

"Shale, let me introduce you to my mother, Mari."

I never knew her mother's name.

"Hi," I said softly.

Mari grinned. "I'm glad you're okay. Rachel has talked so much about you, I feel like I already know you."

Rachel leaned over and hugged me. "I'm glad you're okay, too."

Mother's eyes glistened with tears. "Shale, I realize now who your real friends are—and mine."

"What do you mean?"

"Mari and Rachel did everything they could to help us when we couldn't find you. I was wrong not to let you go over to their apartment."

I stared at my mother. Perhaps more happened when I was in the seventh dimension than I realized.

"And I was wrong also," Mari said, "to believe the rumors."

"What rumors?" I asked.

Rachel spoke up. "When you went missing, Judd came to me and confessed what he did—he thought you ran away because of him. Guilt was eating at him on the inside. He needed to tell someone, and he knew I was your best friend."

"Wow! I can't believe he told you." Three sets of eyes stared back at me. "Did you tell your mother what he said? Or mine?" Part of me hoped she did, and part of me didn't.

"Not exactly," Rachel said. I told Mother that he confided the nasty truth to me, and Mother suggested I talk to Doctor Silverstein in confidence."

"What does that mean?"

"It means he doesn't go around telling everybody."

"Oh."

Mother added. "We decided to hire Doctor Silverstein. He understands you better than anyone else. We want what's best for you—and Judd. He needs help, too. And now he'll get it."

I nodded, but remained quiet.

"Come. Let's get the door open. I hope you'll come in," Mother said, speaking to Rachel and Mari.

We moved out of her way.

"Just for a minute, though, Shale. Remember what the doctor said. You need to rest."

Home never felt so sweet. Mother was back to being Mother, although I could tell something was different.

Inside, I plopped down on the sofa. Remi had picked up some milk and bread on the way home and stuck them in the refrigerator.

I sat wide-eyed gazing at Rachel.

"Why are you looking at me like that?" Rachel asked.

"I've lots to tell you."

"You do?"

I examined the living room and fond memories returned. "I'm so glad to be home."

Mari left us and went into the kitchen.

I pulled the egg out of my dress pocket.

"What's that?" Rachel asked.

I opened it and lifted out the rabbits. After setting the mother bunny down with the two small ones, one of them winked at me.

I gasped. "Did you see that?"

"It winked," Rachel said.

"Yes."

Remi came and sat beside me on the edge of the sofa. "Shale, can I get anything for you? Books, CD's?"

"Yes."

"What's that?

"I want a Bible."

"A Bible?"

Mother frowned, walking into the living room from the kitchen. "We don't have one, do we, Remi?"

Rachel grinned. "I have a Bible, sort of, but it's in Hebrew."

"No, I want a Bible in English. They have them in English, don't they?"

Remi laughed. "I'm sure they have a Bible in any language you want. We'll get one for you tomorrow," Remi promised.

Mari interjected. "We have one you can have, Shale, if it's okay with your parents."

"Sure," Remi said.

"I'll go home and get it now. I'm not even sure where it came from."

I reflected on how similar Rachel's mother was to Mari in the seventh dimension.

I reached down and patted Much-Afraid. "We can keep her, right?"

"Yes, we'll work it out with the apartment manager." Mother paused. "Maybe we could name her Gypsy."

"Gypsy? What do you think, Much-Afraid?"

She barked. "A rose by any other name would smell as sweet."

I laughed. Truly, whatever we had bound in the seventh dimension was bound here, too.

"Where is the stone?" I looked around the living room. In my absence, someone cleaned the apartment. All the boxes were gone.

Mother furrowed her brow. "You want that rock? We left it on the front porch."

"Can you bring it to me?"

"Bring that dirty thing into the house after all the cleaning I've done? If you want that yucky rock, you get it yourself and keep it in your room."

"Let's go get it," Rachel said excitedly. "I want to see it."

We walked outside and found it in the grass a few feet from the front door. Rachel picked it up and lugged it upstairs to my bedroom.

"Where should we put it?" I asked.

"How about your nightstand? The rock isn't that big."

"Sounds good to me." It wasn't dirty either. In fact, it was quite beautiful now that it was off the forest floor, where we could appreciate its beauty.

"Is it magical?" Rachel whispered. "Like the rabbit?"

I chuckled. "Everything is magical in the seventh dimension. I can't wait to tell you about it."

Along the top of the rock, the word Ebenezer appeared, carved into the stone. I smiled at Rachel.

"Magical," we said in unison.

NEXT BOOK IN SEVENTH DIMENSION SERIES

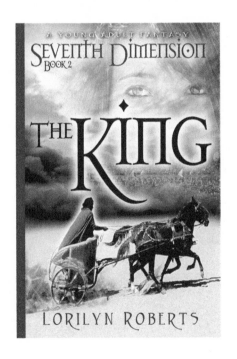

ALSO BY LORILYN ROBERTS

LorilynRoberts.com

Children of Dreams

As an Audiobook

Tails and Purrs for the Heart and Soul

As an Audiobook

ᎢHE ᎠONKEY ᎯND ᎢHE ᏦING
(A Story of Redemption)

Lorilyn Roberts
Illustrated by Linda S. DiFranco

Look for the hidden word "good" on every page.

The Donkey and the King: A Story of Redemption

"Wonderful story with positive Christian values. Loved the illustrations. It's a hit with my kids!"

—"Goodreads" reader

Young readers become world leaders.

Book Love

"Book Love is beautiful inside and out. Roberts uses a child to teach children the love of books and it works beautifully. This book is a must for elementary classrooms and libraries. I highly recommend Book Love by Lorilyn Roberts if you have a child wanting to learn to read."

—Joy Hannabass, Readers' Favorite Reviewer

SEVENTH DIMENSION SERIES

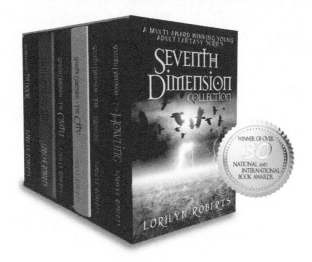

LorilynRoberts.com

Seventh Dimension - The Door, Book 1

As an Audiobook

Seventh Dimension - The King, Book 2

As an Audiobook

Seventh Dimension - The Castle, Book 3

As an Audiobook

Seventh Dimension - The City, Book 4

As an Audiobook

Seventh Dimension - The Prescience, Book 5

Audiobook coming

Seventh Dimension - The Howling, Book 6

As an Audiobook

ADDITIONAL BOOKS

LorilynRoberts.com

Food for Thought Cookbook

Seventh Dimension Devotional Series: Am I Okay,God?

Born-Again Jews - companion book to *Seventh Dimension - The King* - coming

ABOUT THE AUTHOR

 When not writing books, Lorilyn provides closed captioning for television. She adopted her two daughters from Nepal and Vietnam as a single mother and lives in Florida with many rescued cats and a dog.

Lorilyn has won over thirty-five awards for the *Seventh Dimension Series*. She graduated Magna Cum Laude from the University of Alabama with a bachelor's degree in social sciences/humanities that included an emphasis in Biblical history with on-site study in Israel. She received her Master of Arts in Creative Writing from Perelandra College. She is also an amateur ham radio operator. KO4LBS.

If you enjoyed *Seventh Dimension - The Door, Book 1*, please consider posting a short review on your favorite book website. Reviews help authors a great deal, and they are the best way to spread news about a book. Thank you for your interest and support.

Made in United States
Orlando, FL
26 October 2022

23858542R10146